The Love Life
of an
Assistant Animator

& Other Stories

Katherine Vaz

TP

TAILWINDS PRESS

The following images are copyright © 2017 by Katherine Vaz: "My
Labyrinth, with Children" (detail, FIG. 1), "Dog Star" (detail, FIG. 2),
"The White Knight Lifts Away" (detail, FIG. 3), "I Bathe in Water That
Burns Like Ice" (detail, FIG. 4), "Where Did You Lie" (detail, FIG. 5),
"Luck Would Have It" (detail, FIG. 6), "Autograph Without Myself"
(detail, FIG. 7). "Prize, in a Foreign Tongue" (detail, FIG. 8) is from the
archives of Katherine Vaz.

Tailwinds Press
P.O. Box 2283, Radio City Station
New York, NY 10101-2283
www.tailwindspress.com

Published in the United States of America
ISBN: 978-0-9967175-6-4
1st ed. 2017

Table of Contents

CHRISTOPHER CERF

and for my mother, ELIZABETH SULLIVAN VAZ,
a lifelong avid reader

I dreamt in girlhood that I was a ballerina panicky to find the stage. Every door I opened—kitchen drawers, bureaus, the massive portals to the houses of strangers—I found only a burning blue ready to eat me alive. The color of ice at its coldest; the color of stone painted with sky; the color of the dot in the seat of every flame. The color of jungle animals lumbering in dusk; the shade of tired blood. And then I knew it was the flight of ballerinas I longed for, because I imagined their bodies soared past the rules of dying on the earth.

THE LOVE LIFE OF AN ASSISTANT ANIMATOR

- desire + the desire for children to be safe

FIG. 1 (BACK). *One day I built a many-chambered house where I wanted to tuck every child, in a little way with quiet music, under the shelter of its wings.*

Bébé Marie Springs from the Box

Joseph sits hunched over, eating a cake with blue-icing roses from the grocery store. Despite his mother's hollering, he stocks the refrigerator with pastries oozing jelly. She nags him about his clippings of ballerinas and movie stars on the kitchen table, and he ignores her until he can't take any more, and he shouts back.

His crippled brother, Robert, in a wheelchair, draws pictures of the Mouse King. Joseph wishes to protect children. The defenseless.

A grown man, a virgin, he falls into his mind and shudders: Ballerinas are leaping throughout this cramped house. Men hold them so that their legs can go this way and that, dancing in space.

When he leaves his home in Queens and goes into Manhattan, he streaks through the air with other men and women on the Elevated Train.

*

Girls who dash through parks are goddesses.

The desire for wonder is truly as fantastic as wonder itself. Joseph Cornell turns a corner to see what's lying in wait. Old film. A bit of tulle. A teaspoon of sand. A soap-bubble pipe suggesting all is light and breaks in an instant, changing back into thin air, into nothing. Made out of someone's breath, exhaled hard. A toy parakeet: Many of the discards suggest flight. Fame is a type of flight, too—elevation, the elation of seeing from above.

He does box-art. He believes that the new American art form must center upon arranging fragments, the making of shrines to childhood, to loss of innocence, to desire that's childlike or to grown-up erotic pain, framed, behind glass. Eggs, empty vessels. Swans, whose best arias are right before they die.

Time-jumping is another of his hungers. How else can he be a friend with Stéphane Mallarmé, another loner with talent and plagues, far away in another decade in Paris?

Joseph Cornell simply sets a coil spring in a wooden box and calls it "Blériot," after the first man to fly across the English Channel.

*

A child's bubble pipe holds and sprays and dribbles eternity.

A flashcube awaits the capturing of a woman's portrait; how can anyone stroll past a display of flashcubes and not be doubled over with aching? He lines them up—icy diamonds in a velvet box.

Back home in Queens, his mother yells at the mess of film he's cutting to pieces. He has a crush on Rose Hobart, an actress from a B-grade jungle movie, *East of Borneo*, which he found in the trash behind a warehouse in New Jersey. Joseph finds these abandoned items because he's all exposed nerves, and hidden objects rise up, exposing their nerve endings right back at him.

He discards the action sequences. Using Scotch tape, he splices together only Rose's expressions—fear, astonishment, courage, longing—with celluloid fragments of an eclipse. He carts his own projector into Manhattan for the premiere of his homage to Rose Hobart. She's bathed in blue from a tinted lens; her eyelids open and close in distillations of emotion.

*

Salvador Dalí is in the audience and froths in a rage, yelling that he should have created this. He knocks over the projector, mystifying Joseph: When on earth has he ever made another man jealous?

The naked model looks at her friend. She's undressed so that he can paint her portrait. She sits on a plain white block and studies her bare feet—scarlet—it's cold in New York—and her nipples are erect. The painter has brought

7

along a fellow artist, Joseph Cornell, an odd duckling with a shock of hair on an oversized head. He refuses to fully enter the studio with the naked model, preferring to collapse into a chair near the ceiling-to-floor curtain white and billowing as a parachute. He wheezes as if he's going to die, his breathing going in and out of his tightened bellows.

"Does he have asthma?" the model whispers.

The painter does not know Joseph well; only that everyone envies his vision. His box-art is its own school. The boxes contain fear for how the world harms children and child-like adults; they are tableaux of the loss of innocence and the treacheries of yearning. They are about beauty, solitude, desperation to fly, to connect. No one else is constructing dreams out of objects so profoundly basic and real that the dream vanishes into reality dreamed into the depths.

*

"Asthma," says the portrait artist. "Sure."

But the model and her friend know that Joseph is tormented. Fantasies make him writhe and breathe the way a man sounds when he is in love, making love. He cannot control himself. He has never married his cravings to anything this real. It is the first time he is seeing an actual naked woman.

The girl he's hired to straighten out his massive files—his clippings on opera, movies, clothing, machines, French artists, French authors—is frightened. She dislikes his yelping mother and quiet, invalid brother. Buttered pastries and half-eaten junk from Woolworth's are the only food in the house, and she's starving. In the basement where the famous artist works, she finds that he's forgotten to hide his pornography: Pink flesh, glistening labia, and buttocks are held out at the ready; women with their tongues offered as they finger themselves or clutch their breasts.

The girl gazes at his bins of doll parts. Arms, legs, heads, torsos. Suddenly she's in the Frankenstein's lab that exists in every house in America: Always there's a dream of love and its fragments. Always there's the dream of putting the dream of love into a whole created body.

*

She runs. She never returns.

Joseph Cornell's influence is such that he arranges for a showing of his brother Robert's drawings. Suffer the little children . . .

After Robert and their mother die, Joseph often does not get out of his bathrobe as he walks in the small box of the house in Queens. He cries. He writes nasty letters to curators. He's been allotted more than enough pain for a dozen men. These, he reports, are the days of his Bathrobe Wanderings.

In *Untitled (Bébé Marie),* a doll's porcelain face stares through a thicket of brambles. Her body is a flaccid sack. How without massive injury can she get out of her box, past those dry sticks?

Late in life, Joseph cannot achieve intercourse with a woman, but he finds physical love. He tells a friend he is alive now to the miracle of kisses and "soixante-neuf." One of his angels is a Japanese artist, Yayoi. A photograph exists of white-haired Joseph with this girl at his breast. His hand rests lightly on the top of her head, as if she might burst like a soap bubble if he clutches her. He does not care that she might only be here because he's even more famous now. Dreams are useless unless they are housed in a moment like this. He is stunned that a beautiful young girl has her head upon his heart.

Joseph Cornell constructs a collage called *"(Untitled) Time Transfixed,"* of an angel guiding a train out of a dead fireplace.

*

Laurel Thornton has the battery stolen from her car—the third time this month. Her tiny house with its second-hand furniture, remnants, found items, is squeezed between two gangs vying for control of the Westside of Los Angeles—the Santa Monica 13 and the Sotel 13. Laurel is tempted to spray-paint on her outside wall: *You can both have it. Take it!*

There's a thicket, a mess she can't hack through: On a walk, she discovers her husband, Barton, a flight attendant, sitting in a park, gazing at the women who pass. He's eating them alive. She slinks away. Back home, she can see the imprint of their flesh on his eyes. He smokes marijuana and falls asleep, and she sits alone in the living room, swallowing a scream, fantasizing about men she's never met.

*

She selects volumes from the bookcase, each chapter or story a jewel, a shadow-box. She reads in the bathtub as the soap bubbles burst one by one, leaving her at first too hot and then too cold.

Laurel is a nurse. She helps a little boy, Mikhail, put on his braces and walk between two steel barres. "I love you," says Mikhail. "You're my treasure," she says, and hugs him a bit too hard—he must struggle not to flinch. She waits until she's home *(I must vow to mop the linoleum and shine the faucets once a week, tidy objects, tidy hearts...)* to cry. Often she's in her robe by seven at night.

She shuts her eyes and leaps out of her dingy stucco home to fly back and forth in time—to Paris, to Rome, into the embrace of movie stars, cowboys, young waiters who live in hovels and offer her cigarettes after sex, which she lights up, setting the brambles surrounding her on fire; she finds men in top hats in turn-of-the-century New York who turn into animals behind closed doors and buy her cameos that look striking at her throat, and starved as she is, that's enough affection to propel her forward, and midway between the old, conjured past and the time of her being shut up with Barton the glazed-eyed flight attendant in a box in L.A., she meets a portrait artist, who says he must capture her naked, and she undresses swiftly, gratefully, but sitting there watching is a friend of his, an odd bird breathing hard on his perch, so frazzled that he seems ready to crack like a porcelain dove under a fist, and before she can say, "Come here, I'm dying to hold onto you," the portrait painter says, "Laurel, I should paint the two of you entwined, since that's Joseph Cornell, the box-artist, the resident of Queens, the time-traveler, the guardian of fragments, the patron saint of American loneliness."

With acknowledgements to *Utopia Parkway: The Life and Work of Joseph Cornell,* by Deborah Solomon.

Blue Flamingo Looks at Red Water

That bus is going to slam into my daughter. In my stop-action memory, everything lies bare a grace-note before it happens. The school bus grinds forward stupidly, a yellow hippo. Henry is at the crosswalk as I turn the corner across the street to meet them. He is not holding Mary's hand. I'm forever saying, *Remember to hold onto her.* She bolts—toward the cat across the room, the crocus past the fence. She unfastens from me, too, and I have to catch her. In my arms she gets vehement and fights like a fish. We chose the name "Mary" because it is plainspoken, classic, but after she was born, I looked it up: It means *rebellion.* Even while she floated in me, her thighbones twitching like fire-making sticks to produce her fiery skin, she was already a grace-note ahead of being herself, rising out of the skeletal place where our names store their lost meanings.

My hand goes up in a half-wave and half a jabbing to indicate that he must get a grip on her. (Only the stop-action reveals that the warning comes before the greeting.) We are going to Belinda's Crafts, because Mary loves tempera paints. Henry is tired from long hours at Ketchum & Doherty, where he is a paralegal. He has recently completed the task of placing his father, riddled with Alzheimer's, into an open spot in Sunrise Homes. I have finished teaching my geography seminar at Redwood University. After visiting Belinda's, we will stop at Jun's for Korean barbecue. Mary is five years old. She considers it a wonder, the wet green seaweed.

For a fractured second (not available to the naked eye: I detect it only when I run the film on its slowest speed), Henry takes in a pretty blonde going down Jasmine Street and then turns to wave back at me while I scream, "Mary!" She can't wait. She wants to be at Belinda's, she's on to painting the next picture. Memory has lifted away the sound of the impact; horror first thrusts into the nostrils. The brew of rubber, the ether of exhaust. I smell rather than hear the wail of the driver. It's all milk and oil. She's fat and lurching about, like the dybbuk of the bus let loose from the bus. Henry jumps back. It's a twitch of an instinct, because then he aims himself forward, but I'm there first. I run with that voidance of time that puts you in the place you can see before you should land there, and I'm ahead of Henry—how could that happen?—and leaning over her. He's reaching around me; he's tall and makes a shell for me to tuck inside, but I'm the animal with her probes out. Red stripes cover her, but there's an explosion of blood with my hands in the middle of it. Henry must have pulled me away; I must have stood. Because everything's gone now. It is only later that Mary's voice finds me: *Blue sky. Yellow bus. Me in red, Mother.* I had been teaching her that out of the primary colors, all pictures can be made.

I'm slower than you are, Isabel, Henry likes to proclaim, and he is. Slower to get out of a car, to add up sums, to get ready for a party, slower at recollections. I loved it once, that slowness—it used to embody—I remember—care in arranging items in the trunk of a car, the tea-ceremony approach to living; care in brushing my hair, slowly, until it knocked me out; slowness in kissing me.

I want her buried at sea. Cold penetrates me while I sprinkle her into the San Francisco Bay. I'm wearing an apricot dress and my stockings with the black dragons, the ones Mary admired. Mary in the fire, then Mary in the water; Mary red, then Mary blue. Where is Henry? He's on the boat, but I don't see him until we're back in our tiny bungalow for the wake and he's setting out meats and hardening bread slices, fingers of carrots, a knife stuck in mustard. I'm quaking from the chill, and Henry reaches for me and I shudder. My colleagues and neighbors are not bad people, but the effort of trying not to say, "Promise you'll let us know if there's anything you need—" causes Lucille, an assistant professor, to offer a curious variation. "Isabel," she says, "aren't you part Mexican?" I know what she means: cha-cha-cha happiness, cha-cha-cha grief. Why aren't I screeching? We've seen them on newsreels, those women with their ululations, writhing over a coffin. But after shrieking "Mary!" there isn't anything left to yell.

What's pounding the cage of my insides is a whisper. Henry is on his third beer. The wave that comes out of me hits him a glancing blow, because his head rears back, and he opens another beer: *Can't you remember anything? I told you not to let her go.*

The barber who sees that King Midas has sprouted the ears of a jackass crawls outside, digs a hole, and whispers into it, "King Midas has the ears of a jackass!" He covers up the hole.

I walk outside. A bird-of-paradise guards our lawn and the St. Joseph's Coat roses. I say to no one, "You forget everything."

The barber is stunned when the plants exude the chant, "King Midas has the ears of a jackass," grass echoing to grass, and the whisper goes inside everyone until it bursts from their mouths.

The guests leave and there's only Henry and me, two middling souls, bloated and weary. We have made love twice in the past three months. A run through a dragon on my leg makes him look beheaded. The whisper blows in from the wide outdoors where I left it and scrawls itself in the air, in plain view.

Henry disappears for one day. His own whisper erupts: *I shouldn't have let her go. You sit there without a word of comfort. It could have been you.*

In Henry's absence, Simon and Lana, friends from the art department, arrive with an ancient DVD of *The Terminator*. They are married and work together on kinetic sculptures; they win grants to bring discarded bits and pieces to life, and then they drink up the outraged howls. Lana favors velvet dresses and mud-caked Army boots. "Isa-bella-donna," says Simon, hugging me. The three of us laugh ourselves sick at Arnold Schwarzenegger's murder of the entire planet.

I am alone in bed in the afternoon when Henry returns. He stretches out next to me, and I don't release the new whisper but it's that fast into the earth and through the trees, exhaled by the leaves: *I can't touch you.* We even hold hands, a sad little unity but the only one we have, because we both hear it at exactly the same time.

The arrival of Jacob Meyers to our bereavement group one Saturday morning causes a shifting, a discomfort and excitement. Even in a basement at Redwood University, there is a ranking and collating, an assessment of celebrity, a hierarchy stuck like a ramrod into the wet mess of pain. Jacob Meyers is a single father, a famous attorney whose eleven-year-old girl, Dawn, was tortured and left disemboweled near the highway toward Sacramento. Betty—her infant died after his insides refused to grow—scurries to get Jacob some coffee. She has given up asking me where Henry is. He says, "Those people didn't know Mary, so I don't want to know them." I am not beyond admiring that.

Jacob takes the cup from Betty. He's tall and hesitant, dark and sharp-featured, and where most men seem to be a head and hands and their clothing, he is a body barely contained inside what he is wearing. He was in the search party that found Dawn. He offers a detail that we did not know from the newspapers. Betty gasps, and hands fly to mouths, when he says, "A rabbit had jumped onto Dawn." Dawn, brutalized, was still offering a living thing on top of herself. I understand for the first time that line, "Every angel is terrible." I burst out with, "She was lovely!"

My words cleave the room. Coffee quivers seismically in people's Styrofoam cups. Betty may swoon and Andrew, whose son died of cancer, might strangle me. Right as I am about to apologize, Jacob says, "Yes, thank you." He's about to grasp the words that will destroy the grotesqueness, and he says, "It was ingeniously sweet, what she did, holding on to something alive, that's it, that's Dawn."

The meeting does not last long. Jacob is in the hallway as I walk toward the ladies' room. His hand is on the water fountain but suddenly it is too much to bow for a drink, and I put my hand on his inclining back and say, "I—"

It is such a short distance to lean into him as he leans into me. We open our mouths onto each other to deliver the words coming from my throat and the ones coming from his.

We go to the Pine Resort Motel on the Redwood Highway. I hold onto his arm while he drives, and he pulls me toward him in a way that lifts me off the seat. Inside our room, that is the marvel of him. I stay lifted up. The carpet is worn in spots down to its beige grid; aerosol lavender makes a dome over a staleness of smoke. He presses me against the wall to kiss my neck and my hands are all over him, and I say, *Wrap my legs around you, won't you please.* I am thoroughly in the air. I used to try to guess, Is it the man trying to crawl to the underside of a woman's hide, or the other way around? With Jacob gliding in and out of me and me pouring wet down the front of his thighs, I am amazed that I've never seen that it's meant to be both at the same time. All that desire, rammed up against cauterized endings on nerves, constantly in need, deadened in order to get through the day: Is everyone like this, I wonder—and still do. I think yes. Flail off my skin. Kiss me until I feel teeth. Crack open my chest. Ravish me.

We collapse together asleep, and then, holding onto each other, we go into the bathroom to take turns peeing, like an old married couple. It is time to go home. Out in the light, we blink. Highway and rushing cars, blue and red and yellow, with the landscape faint but filling in.

Where am I, what's here? Where is my daughter, so that I can talk to her? Not about this. About our need to watch out for each other, since I'm given to bolting, too.

Jacob leads me to his car, opens the passenger's side for me, and walks to the driver's side. I don't want to have us over by climbing in. When his hand sweeps the hair out of his eyes, it becomes that first gesture we make in the morning, coming to, recalling ourselves. He tilts toward me, and it seems like forever for him to get close. My head rests against his shoulder. I like his tallness, and his disaster-area of hair, his dark eyes. I like all of what he is, down to the history of himself that even he doesn't know. Tremors are still going through him. I put my hand on his chest, and they are there, too, the remainder of loving me, the great, fine habit of the body to retain its standout hours. His fingers go through my hair to get to my scalp. "I didn't hurt you, did I?" he says. "I don't mean to hurt you."

There's only us with throbbing stars crowning our veins. The sky is getting swabbed with erasers. I'm blindingly, out of my skin in love. "It isn't hurt I'm feeling," I whisper. He kisses where the water pours out of my hairline, as if there's a fissure there.

"Oh, sweetheart, I'm so sorry," he says, "It is. That's what it is."

He adds that I'm pretty as a picture and says, I won't forget this. I won't forget you.

I elicit a promise: Will he call me every year on my birthday? Let's see how well we manage to fit time over today.

He says Yes, he won't fail to remember.

But in the night, knives come at me and worry openings I didn't know I had, and I'm leaking everywhere. Henry comes home late from work, while I'm sleeping, and calls the next morning to say, "Were you drunk? You wet the bed. I thought that was my job, wet dreams."

I say, "Getting drunk is your job," and I hang up on him.

How can you go on? That's the implied question whenever an outstretched hand hovers near my skin, wary that mere touch might detonate me. People don't mean to be cruel. They're just not lucky. No Mary or Dawn to reveal to them that memory seems to run backward to disguise its yearning to stream forward. I live in a constant thrill: What will Mary do next? Life torques the drives begun in childhood, makes them oblique—her vehemence might convert itself into a romantic fervor, the kind usually doomed and hidden. She comes to me with her eyebrows—black and heavy like mine—plucked in a thin line, in the throes of the lifelong project of badly taming herself. Why does it persist, this invented memory of Mary wearing a mortarboard and graduation gown, this perpetual finding her on some verge? It seems to grow out of Mary in her water wings in the backyard pool. I ask Henry if he thinks Mary would have been a swimmer as good as he is, and he stares at me before he says, "She already was." Henry has his sadder twist; he can't dream her forward, has left her stuck in time.

It works backward, too, memory; it revises the past we are foolish to think never alters. I was born in Mexico City and lived there until I was seven. My father, Inocéncio, was an electrician who played the harp. He hated that people thought only of faraway angels when it came to such a wonderful instrument. To have it speak of us as we were truly living, he wrote a solo about a man in Mexico City steering his harp on a bicycle through traffic. He wore driving gloves while performing on stage, while a tape of blasting horns, shattering glass, and screeching brakes built the harmony.

I would in fact ride with him in traffic while he transported his harp, a Veracruzian *jarocho*, on a bicycle we'd bought from the baker, with an enormous front basket. We wobbled past buses with riders hanging out of the doors, past swerving green cabs; once we rammed into a man steering a red toy wagon filled with piglets. A friend with a chestnut cart liked to pelt us with uncooked chestnuts when we passed his corner, which made my father roar with laughter and almost crash us as we headed into the Alameda Central with its booths of the Magi and Snoopy dolls, maize leaves, clay whistles, and amplifiers. My father kept shouting, "Here we go, Mechita!" My middle name is Mercedes, and he found my nickname there, because I was thin and quick-tempered and *mecha* is also the wick of a candle. I recall being fearless. It was all of my native country for me: father, harp, little items to discover at the bazaar, a baker's bicycle heading through traffic, people with their lives dangling every which way. A *fullness* reigned there, cracks in walls sprouting ivy with wood spiders hanging from the ivy's leaves, a perilous decorative brimming, disaster taking a long time in front of a mirror while putting on its hat; everyone trailing bits and pieces, everything bendable or easy to shatter, like vertebrae.

Mary lived only the years she would never have remembered, so I invite her in to revise what I think I know. She insists that my father is not shouting, "Here we go!" but "Hold on, hold on!" The past changes, thanks to her: I'm clutching my father's *guayabera* shirt until I feel skin because I must hold on, and I'm holding on, holding on, danger spilling past me, holding on to my father and the daughter not yet born, Mary Gomez Eisenberg. My name is tucked into the middle of her. My father died not during but after his "Angeles de la Calle" solo, not in traffic but in his bed, of a heart disease. My Irish, Texas-born mother moved us to San Francisco, where she had a sister. Henry had a Jewish father and a Norwegian mother, and when we were first married, we joked about his mother's gods in their severe costumes. Mary was our prediction of a new, hybrid rule. We did our part to knock the world out of its obsession with tribal purity.

On my first birthday after I leave the bereavement group, Jacob Meyers calls and says, "Tell me what you're doing."

I am putting away a box of Mary's paintings. I have recently taken them down from the walls. (I didn't keep her clothing or furniture, things another child might need.) My favorite is the one I call "Blue Flamingo Looks at Red Water." In its frame, the blue flamingo under glass is gazing into a red pool at its reflection. The water is giving its tones to the bird, and the bird has lent its color to the water.

"I'm looking at her blue flamingo looking at red water," I say.

"That's good," he says.

"Tell me what the year has brought you," I say.

He tells me he is writing a book.

22

On my second birthday after the accident, Jacob Meyers calls and says, "Have you found Henry again?"

They are only now returning to me, people orbiting around objects—streets, strata, names, all of which should matter to a teacher of geography. Simon and Lana foraging with me in the junkyards for bizarrely shaped iron. Henry as I watch him go out the door with his orange bag of swimming gear, on his way to the Olympic pool on the corner; Henry going gray while slumbering in his chair while the night is still young. How could I have married a man twelve years older than I am without imagining this time would come? Redwood, white-hot in summer, the flanks of dogs marinated with the oil of the wild mint, the red plastic cups in the gutter from the kegger parties, town versus gown, California's affection for giving its streets self-loathing names, Yale, Harvard, Cornell. Henry sitting at Roma Café, denying that he is gazing at girls. But when I study his corneas, the images are stuck there, scrapes of sexual fandango, girls going upside down on trapezes. The forty-year-old geography teacher who gave up the idea of being a photographer and the fifty-two-year-old paralegal who was never a lawyer, the late-bloomers, late parents, mildly, slowly—with Henry's slowness—going toward erosion. The second glass of wine topped off heavily, so that the next glass could be thought of as a third and not a fourth; the game show after the evening news, eroding further into an addiction to police shows. Ending a marriage isn't easy. You hack it to pieces, but the pieces sprout into tiny replicated bodies of the marriage, bleeding onto your shoes.

I go to our bedroom, a bursting-from-the-seams place, books and clothing piled on the floor, T-shirts over the backs of the rickety chairs that Henry saved from college and never replaced. That I never replaced either. Henry lies asleep, kneading the sheet in his hands the way people do in hospitals right before they die, as if retreating under a winding cloth. I shout, "Henry? Henry!" His grip on the sheet alarms me, and I kneel on the bed, tugging it away from him. He fights for the cloth—white with sprigs of violets, my selection, not his; how many men lie down in the woman's choice?—and I fight back and succeed in pulling it away. There is a cushioning of beer under his skin, up and down the length of him. It's a light and foamy thing; the beer pooled under there without any conversion, pausing only to wick anything alive out of his hair, which used to be blond. Now it's straw. Here's my answer; this is why his eyes have yellowed.

"Oh, Henry," I say, my palm on his chest. He pulls me to him, and that quickly I am below him and he is inside me, clinging so ferociously I can't move. "Henry?" I say. He's crushing me; I don't have a sensation of my chest, only of my bare ribcage. It's not Henry's face pressing all over mine, but the weight of the skeleton in his face; it's the bones I feel as he suffocates me with kisses. I have an image of the jangling man from biology class, hanging by a thread to teach us femur, clavicle, butterflied plate of pelvic bone. I kiss him back because I am too sad not to. He thinks all is forgiven—and it is, because I am suddenly aware that this is what I've been building toward: I want to cut the last tie that will keep me from going into indifference. Because this isn't love, this is a determination to reinstate it through impact. I only want him to release me. I struggle, and that is enough of a response for him to moan my name. I am crying. He kisses away my tears.

Still he holds on; his pressure won't relent. I stroke his back with my hand. And I take back, frightened, the notion of indifference: If it is not love, it is compassion soaking into me, and that, after all, is not a far tangent from the thing itself, though we may never get back to it.

In the morning we rest against each other, without speaking. He buys me walking shoes, and I train climber roses, tea-sized crimson, up the front of our bungalow. He gives me blank books with elaborate covers of antique maps or Victorian clocks. That's the old Henry, as he was when I first met him, generous, suffering a hundred details on my behalf, taking two hours one day to break my wrong timing of frog-kick to breaststroke in the pool, and I was generous right back, thinking up ways to thank him.

His oddest gift now is an intensification in his silence; every now and then, he flinches. It is what I am missing about Mary: He tells me that he's stuck with living the sensation of impact. His frame takes the hit of it; he goes to it and winces, while I pull up short; I can't go where he's going, but it's some recollection of the last of Mary, and I'll try to draw closer to it. The doctor said that Mary hadn't felt a thing. Mary? Feeling nothing? What is that split-second like, to have your body crushed, your head against metal—what is the enormity of that pain? The mastodon against the bobbling wind chime of a child's skeleton.

I don't know how to rescue Henry from this. I would like to substitute the feel of crashing with sounds of sad beauty. I download songs by the Portuguese *fado* singer Mísia. *Fados* are the traditional songs of fate, mournful; Mísia has a Louise Brooks haircut and full lips and is said to bring a new tone to this music of the past.

Henry thanks me but does not play the songs again, at least not with me present.

He hangs paper fish on the patio and calls it the Inland Sea. My arm around his waist, I say, "Thanks, Henry. It's pretty." I don't mind that the wind comes in and shreds the fish. We watch pieces of the lobster being carried away. Red dots will land on far places, and no one will guess that the specks are lobsters from an Inland Sea. I stop. For the first time, I can identify a moment, watching the lobsters, when Mary—or is it Henry?—gives me the relief of not contemplating her.

But it is Henry who clings more and more to the relief of not dwelling upon Mary: The pieces of him are going sailing I have no idea where.

I say, "Remember when I took this photo?" Redwood no longer has any redwood trees, but there was once one so huge that when they sawed it down, they polished the stump into a dance floor. We dressed Mary in her green shift, and I let her wear my clip-on shell earrings and red lipstick, and we went to a fancy party there. I snapped a picture of Mary blowing kisses, surrounded by women in evening dress and pearls and men in suits who had also come to whirl around on the chopped-off neck of the King of Trees. Henry had disappeared in the crowd.

"Sorry," he says. "Was I there?"

We drive to the Yuletide Farm. Henry takes Road 102; it's as if the valley heat defeated any imagination for naming the byways. (My student Maureen's essay comes to mind: How terrain determines our degree of hope.) 102's redness is brought out by the rain, as if storms have flayed away the pale skin. The Persian-rug colors, gold and crimson, are interrupted by very little—an apiary, a dairy. Milk and honey. (Matthew, who is taking geography because he wants to map the real world, the erosions, depths, rings, and upheavals, not because he's terrible at math or English, writes about the effects of California's crumbling sea-line reaching far inland.)

I am happy; we used to take Mary to the Yuletide Farm, and she'd stamp her feet and dash into the thicket of trees.

"Remember the time that Mary climbed one of the firs?" I ask.

"No, Isabel, I don't," he says, impatient, and I am so furious that we end up leaving our saw in the car and selecting one already cut down. In silence, we tie it to the top of the car in the traditional, slaughtered-deer pose.

Is it willful erasure, an attempt to acquit himself of her? Often his *Sorry, no, no* angers me, and other times I have a guilt that leaves me thinking *to each his own way*: If Mary has selected him and not me to keep reliving the sensation of her last moment, how wearying. No wonder he's exhausted. Then, now, always: He's left wanting her to stop.

But he starts saying *stop* to me, too.

On the third anniversary of Mary's accident, I ask what's on his mind. To me the square of the day on the calendar sits like a jack-in-the-box with its hair-trigger latch: Out springs Mary.

"I'm thinking that maybe you think too much, Isabel," he says.

He surpasses the great three lost items of the quotidian male—keys, glasses, wallet—and now misplaces events. I ask him to make a reservation at a restaurant, and he neglects to do it. I leave out the papers he needs to bring to work, and he overlooks them. *Now what was that fellow's name again? Now what was that? Was that Thursday?* form a refrain that drives me into the bathroom, where I shut the door and splash water on my face to keep from shrieking. He jots down lists before going to the grocery store so he won't forget anything, and then he forgets the list but brings back something he knows I'll like.

I remind him to call Sunrise Homes every week to obtain the routine permission to take his father out for their Sunday breakfasts, and I collect magazines for his father, and Henry leaves them behind. They've been visiting several times a week; are sympathy pains infiltrating Henry? His dad's Alzheimer's has not yet removed recognition of his son, and of course Henry should clutch that slender tie as long as possible. I walk outside to cool off: *You forget everything* is still written in the air, where I first delivered it, circulating on the breeze that stirs the last hanging fragments of the Inland Sea.

At Simon and Lana's, Simon asks Henry if he remembers the night with the coyotes.

"No," says Henry, his voice low and tired.

It has honestly gone out of his head, and I'm startled.

"Sure you do," says Simon.

Lana, cutting the strawberry torte, pauses with the knife and says, "Henry, that was six months ago."

"We were at my brother Patrick's ranch, out in Death Valley," says Simon. He shoots a glance at me, but I have to look away. I stare at their sunflower-patterned tablecloth, dizzy.

"We'd been drinking a lot of beer, and Patrick led us out to piss around the perimeter of the ranch, because he'd heard the scent of human males keeps the coyotes away. We laughed about getting skewed on the cactus spines, remember?"

"Sort of," says Henry.

My foot swings out and knocks a leg of the table. Lana stops cutting the torte. I'm not going to be able to contain myself. I can recall that night down to the low-lying wildflowers, a vibrant purple. Henry and I made love that night with a howling like the furious dead held at bay around the ranch's borders.

"How can you forget that?" I say, more harshly than I should.

"What?" he says.

"Jesus, Jesus Christ!" I shout. "Can't you remember anything?"

Henry is red and subdued. Lana says, "Shh, it doesn't matter."

"It does," I say.

"All right," says Simon. "It's been a long evening. I didn't mean to—"

"You're fine," says Henry. "I'm fine."

I'm going to strangle on the words. *No you're not!*

When we say goodbye, Simon whispers, "Don't worry. It's good to see you both out and around again. That's all."

But it isn't all. In the car, I say, "Henry, what is with you?"

He explodes. "*Nothing.* Nothing is—what did you say?—'with me.'"

"That's right. *Nothing* is with you," I say, and he stares straight ahead, and instead of asking him what's wrong, I start to cry and say, "I'm sorry, Henry."

"For what?" he says, and smiles at me sadly. He squeezes my knee, my outburst already gone from him. He absolves me so readily, as easily as the images in his head dissolve.

When Jacob calls me on my birthday that year, I say, "Tell me what's new with you."

He has finished his book. It is not a rehash of "his case"; he won't offer Dawn for public scrutiny. It's a novel based on his childhood in Idaho, where the Snake River vanishes into a terrace of land. He is a person becoming who he is now by revising what he was. His law practice is doing well. He is getting married, to a violinist who teaches poetry in the schools. Her name is Emily.

"Jacob. I'm so glad." Because it amazes me. At any diminished point, with its impetus toward further diminishing, *life pulls up.* Fresh and strong, a turning away from the wall.

He asks, "What's ahead of you, Isabel?"

I freeze. It's a prompting to lift my head and look at the approaching years: Why have I been so frightened to see Henry? I think I know; I think I've known for quite a while. I figured that with Mary we were so overdrawn with tragedy that it would leave us alone. But time has trickled on, to a present, new dilemma, even if I have not been ready to name it. We pretend that it passes for goodness, what life does, substituting eminent clarity for beneficence.

"Goodbye, dear," I say to Jacob. "I don't know what's ahead. I think I'm afraid to say."

"Will you take care of yourself?" he asks. "Will you take care of Henry?"

Henry arrives home that night with my birthday gift: a certificate for scuba-diving lessons. My affection for water is romantic; I've mentioned that I would like to make it real. He has kept that in mind.

I kiss him. Women often struggle against asking, *What has he done?* when they know they must ask, *Who is he?*

He plays the Mísia tunes on his computer. "I love this album," he says. "Remember how we made love while this played in the background at the ski cabin four years ago?"

A tremor courses through me. I'm quiet instead of saying, "Henry, are you out of your mind? I downloaded that a short while ago. How can you forget? It's new."

He's going on: It's the weekend we like best, our annual winter trip to the mountains. Everyone vanishes inside to watch the Super Bowl. The scenery of pure snow clears away until there's only you and me, and maybe some others. But mostly it's you and me, and the world packed up in white, ready to be stored away, as if then, truly, it would be just the two of us.

He thinks I'm shaking from memory, so he touches my face as I close my eyes. Fifty-two is young, but I can guess the end that is meant for him, and to that end he will now take himself. He has turned toward old age. I shall never know—and now it hardly matters—whether letting go of Mary, the death of her, brought him sooner to the start of this. He has carried from birth the chemical fate of forgetting, the Alzheimer's of his father, the early senility of both his grandfathers and one of his grandmothers. He is not forgetting Mary to avoid pain; he is entering the pain that is famous for not stopping. Is he aware of what is overtaking him? Did I imagine he would escape? Or that there would be some discernible divide—one day

31

whole, the next day in the depths of illness? This fate is not his fault. As befits Henry, it is happening slowly, and that is how I will lose him, instead of full-force and swiftly, like my daughter. I have been too horrified to look at what is true. The dead body of a little girl is not a painting. It is not beautiful. And loss of memory can be a physical fact, death strolling in, grinning and taking its time. Taking its time in telling us, too, that it came to stay when we weren't looking.

Henry has a surprise. On my birthday, I like trying something a little frightening or new, and we run two blocks to the Civic Center pool and steal over the fence, like high school kids. He brings my suit, goggles, and towel but forgets my cap. I tell him not to bother going back for it.

He wants to teach me the butterfly, a stroke I've never mastered. It requires a person to sweep her arms forward as if she's trying to toss her body into its own embrace right as it's time for the next thrust forward.

Like this, like this, he says, telling me to hold onto his neck. I stretch out along his back. Don't let go, he says. His hips arch and descend and mine do too; it's supposed to look obscene, he's told me. When he pauses at the wall and asks if I'd like to try it alone, I say that left to myself, I would drown.

Then hold on, he says, and I put my arms around his neck and lie on his back again. His muscles know so perfectly what to do that they no longer need to remind themselves. His legs pound in the dolphin kick, and his arms circle. I liked this about him the first time I saw him, before knowing his name.

We haul ourselves out and sit, shivering. Henry puts his arm around me along with the towel. The moon is smeared into a white glaze. He says, "Are you going to leave me, Isabel?"

Our hearts are working hard—his for going the distance, mine from the effort of the new motion. The body sends its tired blue blood up to the heart, and there in the divided chambers, hidden but ceaseless, the work goes on, minute by minute, cleaning it to red again. Bless its repetition—bless that old washerwoman, the heart.

Because I have not answered, he asks again merely by announcing my name.

"Isabel?"

Bless Mary's blue flamingo, speaking to me across the years: blue washing its reflection in red water.

"You're always talking about what Mary did," he says. "I only remember who she was. I'm sorry."

"Don't be sorry," I say.

"Her black hair, like yours. Her impatience, like yours. Her hands covered with paint. Her calling out, knowing I'd come running."

I know the truth of what is to come with Henry as he drifts farther into forgetting, and I shall summon the fortitude to bear it to its distant finish. Up to now, I've neither set him free nor loved him enough nor looked clearly at his dying memory. I have been letting go of him with brutal slowness.

"Isabel," he says, "remember our time in St. Louis?"

The two of us are riding a paddleboat on the Mississippi. One dance floor offers rock-and-roll, another ballroom dancing. Another features Big Band music and older couples reliving that sensationally odd look of being festive during wartime. The sunset flattens a replica of itself onto the river: red of sky onto blue of water, then blue-black night sky looking at red water. Stars shrunk to the size of waterbugs are painted on the surface. We have not been married long. Neither of us is a dancer. But we know how to move through water; we'd met and fallen in love while swimming, and here we are still—carried upon this river.

We stumble across something marvelous: The first deck is reserved for a large group of people in wheelchairs. They have come with sponsors who hold onto their hands and wheel them in a dance while the music plays, Bach and the Stones and country-western: the music from all the other floors. Everyone is content to veer without hurry. The faces of those being wheeled are lifted toward the lit-up eyes of the people guiding them around.

"I remember," I say to Henry. "I'd forgotten."

As the Mississippi moves below those different styles and times stacked one on top of the other, we play that game of whispering, Would you love me if I could not walk? Would you kiss me if my hair fell out and I went blind?

Would you still want me? Would you love me if I forgot my name and yours? If I forgot my past and everyone in it? You would have to remember for me that we promised never to leave this behind, this wanting to die of happiness as the wheelchairs circle. The river is slow, and the boat is slower. The porthole windows let in the air as the band plays. Already, before we know her, our daughter comes to greet us with her wild imaginings, because the water is scarlet. The heart is halved. The sky is red and washes blue by morning. We pass by the lighted cities that we will never visit, with their storehouse of invisible lives and lovemaking in unknown rooms, with the blue and the red and the river without let-up making their mysterious sounds while slowly bearing us on.

bebi muito uísque e hoje tenho dores de cabeça. Sinto-a vazia.

East Bay Grease

My daughters are shot dead. I run in my nightshirt toward the metallic banging on the front porch. Finally I beat on Gina enough to make her quit dancing around that gang, but suddenly I'm the one with a crazy woman swearing she'll "get me." If my girls end up hurt *it's all my fault.* I'll gather Gina bleeding in my arms; we'll form a sort of gangland Pietà, and my howling will reach the baby inside her. I've already named my grandchild Annie.

The dawn holds a shower curtain of fog, a splattered thing, as I burst outside. Someone has thrown a wrapped turkey at my door. And canned food: creamed corn, tamales, pumpkin-pie mix, olives. Everything in California is drive-by, even the charity. A car swerved close, pitched this feast at us, and floored the accelerator. When I took Gina and Blanca to get flu shots, we idled in the line of autos, flapped our arms out the windows, and a nurse jabbed us with needles. Gina said, "Unreal, a drive-by shotting." She and I laughed. Blanca gripped her arm as if I'd taken her to have it broken.

The clove-and-roasted-meat smell of Thanksgiving is already tossing its skeins into the air to find the invisible

Fig. 2 (opposite). *I stood in my doorway and saw myself in every restless motion.*

loom over the nation. My blue-striped nightshirt is open to my breasts. Lou drew his last breath in it. It reaches to my knees. He died of a heart attack two years ago, age forty-eight, a simple now-you're-there-now-you're-gone affair. My co-workers at the DMV probably decided I need a holiday consolation and donated the food. Last month, I flunked the written driver's test of a dry little woman named Iris McCarthy, and she opened her purse long enough for me to see her lady's silver pistol glistening. She said I was keeping her from driving to Sacramento to beg her boyfriend not to leave her for someone younger. She stared at my nameplate. "I'll find out where you live," she whispered.

Sometimes I'll notice small things out of place. The doormat turned upside down. The rosemary or sage dug out of the garden.

A can of bouillon rolls against my ankle, and as I stoop I see a bouquet left by the side of the stairs. Maybe the sound that startled me was a florist's van backfiring. With a rustle of cellophane, I lift the armful of gladioli, cream-colored and honey-yellow, to my chest. The unsprouted tips stroke my chin.

The treasures today are coming from near and far: I know which distant man sent the flowers; I don't even need to touch the card to soak his name through my skin.

I live on D Street in Hayward (or Hay-Weird, according to Gina), in a stretch where we are Doing Our Best With What We Have. Trim pastel boxes, hardwood floors. Roof-high cacti, white lions (plaster, from rubber molds). Hibiscus, bonsais with their limbs so solidly pinned they don't scream anymore. Downhill, toward the city's center, the homeowners are more like squatters-for-life. They brood, simmer, and kick volcanic rocks around, and when they stop, they call it a garden. One ex-soldier sprays a gnome of green snow onto his window for Christmas, and who can say if it's fright or cheer. Weeds sprout in the satellite dishes so they turn into hairy armpits, and the birds-of-paradise aim their beaks toward each other's eyes. Up the hill, in the Fairview kingdom with the Arabian Horse Ranch and Lone Tree Cemetery, the houses are gold and strawberry-pink with cupolas. The "Pedestrians on Shoulders" sign shows adults carrying children piggy-back. The silhouetted babies have arms flung around the necks of their parents, everyone's hair flying. When I stare at that sign, I can feel those tiny limbs pressing against my windpipe.

Ever since the shine of that pistol melted my corneas, the picture of Iris in my head easily leaks through my eyes, onto the landscape. I spot her everywhere: shaggy pinecone hair, a mountain lion's squint.

While I'm patrolling our walkway, Gina bangs through the screen door, in a stained football jersey, mascara carving spikes down her cheeks. "What the fuck woke me up?" she hisses. Dried spit cakes her chin; she gets morning sickness. "What's this shit doing at my house?"

Instead of forbidding that filthy talk, I'm excited she's mentioned *her house*. Maybe she's caving in, conceding the argument we started last night. I'd suggested that since she had a high-school diploma pieced together by tape and wishes (who flunks gym twice?), and though it was stupid to get knocked up at eighteen, all the more reason for her to stay at home instead of announcing she's moving out, and Gina had shouted that I wanted to get my hands on her baby to correct my mistakes with her, and I'd screamed, *You bet I do!*

I can't stomach that her idiot stoner boyfriend will raise my grandbaby. In the Hawaiian Tropicana Apartments. Any Californian will confirm that "Hawaii" in a title here (the Aloha Gardens, etc.) guarantees a shithole, possibly a dangerous one.

She's gazing at my flowers as I warble, "So you'll stay with me?"

"Mami, can we not do this now? Jesus. I'm ready to puke again as it is." She reaches for the spray of glads, and I say, "Why would you think these are for you?"

She steps back, swats a can with her foot. I've hurt her. I can't stop. "These couldn't be from The Pineapple"—her boyfriend's name is Martin, but his hair is spiked and he's on what used to be called The Dole, so "The Pineapple" it is—"because that would require him to pick up a telephone and call, actions beyond his organizational powers. And he'd have to pay money."

A Lincoln Continental cruises past with a license-plate holder that reads "310 Motoring." The company that takes its name from the L.A. area code. They trick out the fancy cars of athletes and movie stars. "Oh," Gina whispers, giggling. "Mami! Are the flowers from your famous luuu-vah? Your ee-big, ee-tough boy-man-friend?" She grabs the hem of her football jersey and performs some twisty-thing with her rounded torso. "Hay-seuss, Mami, you screwed up. I coulda had a star for a Papi." She pivots. "Instead of making you little loco nuts the way you are now, I could've been a Hollywood bitch to make you super-size crazy."

I cover my face with my bouquet. Through the gladioli, I peer at her like a hunter grinning in a duck blind. "You and Blanca are going to help your poor widowed mother have a good feast day. Start by doing something with these—" I wave at the cans and the sweating turkey.

She grabs the turkey's leg, dangles it as if it's a hollering brat, and slams inside, leaving me to rip open the gift card on my flowers: *For Brenda. Always wishing you well . . . fondly, X.* He's signed his real name, but I'm afraid you might laugh; you won't believe me, because he truly is a huge star in adventure films and space-age thrillers, all with amazing weaponry. In a dark theater, I've watched him fire two guns backward over his shoulders and hit bad guys sneaking up on him. He was my shy date to the Senior Prom at Hayward High. X bought a camellia for my swept-up hair. Five of the dances were fast, and X knew how to re-pin the camellia. Six of the dances were slow. The theme was Aquatic Wonders, the gym draped in blue and green spirals. The band played Tower of Power's "East Bay Grease" because we were supposed to be proud to be the oily cousins, the Mexicans, Italians, Portuguese, and Greeks, across the dazzling water from San Francisco. X and I held hands when he walked me home, and we kissed. That was the entirety of my time with him. I was leaking-from-my-gills crazy for Lou Márquez, who was out drinking beer with his friends, half of whom were telling him to marry me, already, and the other half were saying he was too young and life was long.

Breezes lift my nightshirt as I check our mailbox— some days I check three, four times. A map of Sacramento was once crammed inside. There's a note addressed to "Brenda, Gina & Blanca: HAPPY HOLIDAY!!!" I

41

crumble the paper, pitch it down the storm drain. *How does Iris know the names of my girls?* I'm hoping the note is from Mr. Ellison, the widower a block away. He stuck one hundred wrapped candy canes into his fried lawn: He asked me sadly why children don't take them.

I can't call the police. A friend of a friend discovered for me that Iris has a handgun permit. The note only says, "Happy Holiday," and it's swimming through the drain. I'd be forced to relive that episode when my planter of hydrangeas had a knife thrust into its dirt. The officer sighed as he said, With the crowd your daughter kept, lady, you fill in that blank, whaddya say? They interviewed my co-workers, who had to admit, No, they hadn't *seen* the pistol, but they completely believed me. Gina's shoplifting, marijuana bust, joy-riding. The cops have been nice, under the circumstances.

The tension gets sharp as needles that impale every pore until you're inside an Iron Maiden. It hurts like to make you see stars.

As I dress, black crewneck sweater and denim skirt, I hide the card from X in my loose-ends drawer under the string, scissors, matches. I don't pine for him. Last month he got an award at the Kennedy Center, and we caught it on television. Gina and Blanca teased me. But X is in the tabloids and sends his ex-wives legal documents. I get cards and flowers, never on a schedule, but without fail once or twice a year.

I carry the glads into the kitchen. Blanca shuffles into view in her sweatpants and that oatmeal cardigan that makes her look like a kitten in a slashed-open bag fished from a river. I want to torch it on Mission Boulevard in front of the Paul Bunyan statue at the tire store. I suspect she's drinking herself sick every night. She's twenty-two, a teller in a bank. I had her when I was nineteen. She confessed, sobbing, that she owes $12,000 on her credit cards. I've told her she can stay at home if she quits buying earrings and sunglasses and going to trendy restaurants (and bars). *Credit cards are the business cards of Satan, Blanca. Why do you kids today need so much junk?*

I say, "Baby? Did you have a bad night?"

Her dyed yellow hair is showing black roots in a band wider than my hand. She's an overboiled noodle, exploded to paste. "What's a good night feel like, Mami?" she asks.

"Like today, baby," I say. "Like tonight. You'll see."

The needles from the Iron Maiden enclosing me are elongating inside. They're becoming arrows below the surface of my skin with nowhere to shoot out. How has it happened that by doing my job decently I have exposed my daughters to harm? While I'm fanning out my glads in a lacquer vase, Blanca hauls the turkey I bought for us out of the refrigerator and groans, "Oh, crap, I forgot to take the bag of weird-ass stuff out of the neck hole before I stuffed this thing." I'd given her one assignment, to be in charge of the turkey. The universe narrows. My sight absorbs the splattered orange-juice-concentrate can I keep by the stove, where I pour bacon fat.

"Blanca? Dear?" I say, not looking at her yet. *"Please tell me you didn't stuff an uncooked turkey and store it overnight."*

Gina strolls in and snorts, "What did fuck-up do now?"

"Gina!" I scream. "I'm about at my limit!"

"Whoo, Ma, okay."

I grab the raw turkey, pull the sack of gizzards from the neck, and yank its legs apart. Wet cornbread dressing is crowning toward me.

"ARE YOU TRYING TO KILL US ALL?"

Blanca and Gina call a truce to their perpetual guerilla warfare in order to exchange glances and shrugs.

"Everyone KNOWS not to stuff a turkey the night before."

"WHY NOT?" shouts Blanca.

"Because *salmonella*, is why not. Sickness. You know—*death*."

"How am I supposed to know that? You never taught us that."

"I didn't teach you a lot of things you've picked up!" Light-headed, I notice that Gina has inked "DGF" on the knuckles of her right hand, and her left hand blazes with "XIV." One is the insignia of the Don't Give a Fuck gang, the other is for the Norteños, because "N" is the four-teenth letter of the alphabet. When they're not buying guns or holding their Tupac-soundalike seminars or designing their fun fashions, they zip around town X-ing out each other's tags on fences. X, X, X. Bang, bang, bang. I grab her wrists and haul her hands toward my face. "Gina? GINA?" I start to flat-out plain bawl.

"Ma! Martin and me were horsing around! You know, writing on each other and shit. I told you, I don't run with those clowns anymore, Martin's out of it, too." She flings an arm around me. "Come on, Mami, don't cry!" Blanca is glaring at the turkey and whining about doing a chore on time for once and I should be happy maybe.

My girls got their father's Mexican skin. I'm only half-Greek on my mother's side; the rest is a custard of

Irish, English. Gina and Blanca are ashamed of my fairness, though they both look Latina. Blanca is on the pale side, and it makes her mad at me. Gina puts on a short skirt and she's the real item. They have large pores, and as teenagers they'd press their foreheads against brown-paper bags and hold the translucent blot up to the light. My freckled skin is thinning to crepe. I wear dot-pearl earrings; they love those chandelier styles that drip and swing. It's funny they hoot that I'm a fool for not trapping X, because then they wouldn't be Latina at all, and I can't imagine them otherwise; they wouldn't be so foreignly mine.

I'm digging the heels of my hands into my eyes to dry my tears, but I suppose it seems I'm trying to blind myself, and Gina tugs them free. Our curtains are stamped with fleur-de-lis; the maple kitchen table has a folded English-muffin carton under its one short leg. The sill offers a line-up of sugar skulls from a Day of the Dead party.

Okay! I'm okay! I thump the charity turkey on the counter. The girls are silent. "No problem!" I say. "We have a new one to stuff right here! So let's see..." and I'm throwing open cupboards... "I bought an extra package of cornbread cubes... where is it?" And where has Gina stored those cans, if they're not on the shelves?

"Mami," says Blanca. "I used both boxes."

Okay! All it means is that one of us gets to join the gleeful throngs thronging at the grocery store, full of their eleventh-hour cheer!

"I already did my job, I'm not going," come the pealing tones from Blanca.

"Yeah, you did it like to poison us, you Lucrezia Borgia bitch," says Gina, who wheels around, opens the lid of the trashcan, and empties her insides so violently I'm afraid the baby will lodge in her throat.

"Good one, whore," says Blanca.

Gina must have been awake in school when the Borgias were stuck into the lesson plans so Hayward kids won't think their own families are so terrible. I try to press a cool palm to her forehead and she shoves me aside, heaves again. I go to hug Blanca, and she growls, Right, kiss up to the murderess.

A note pinned to our corkboard reads, "VIVA YOU TURKEY," the words dripped in glue caked with green glitter. "Where did you get that?" I screech.

Gina straightens, clutching her gut. "From Alicia, Mami. Would you *stop* about some whack job chasing you? You're getting paranoid and freaky and—leave me alone."

The knife in the planter, the mat spun upside down, the breathing smears on the front glass... whenever I warn the girls to be careful, they roll their eyes.

I slide my car down D Street toward Jackson. Keep on Jackson and you'll end up in the ghost spot where the salt flats once thrived, our white gold, beds where the sun drank the water out of the brine. I stick to the center of town, half-deserted: past the saloon with the mural of coyotes yelping and the Cow Palace Diner with the revolving sign of a steer with a crown askew. Lou and I once took the girls there, and they wept at the sawed-off blood vessels in their meat because it hit them that they were chewing an animal.

Emil Villa's b-b-q place, the Captain Aguas Dive Center, the sunlight flinging palomino blotches onto walls: Hayward is Edward Hopper done over Latin. I park at the Carniceria Morelia *(Abarrotes, Verduras, Frutas)*, and forgive it for being adjacent to the pitchfork-studded hell where I earn my keep, the DMV. Scattered throughout the shelves are curios so delicate they're like baby chicks that need warming in the hand: the tray of quail eggs, ten for $1.49. Packets of anise seeds, chili pods, and Siete Azahares. They don't list what the Seven Blossoms are, so I imagine *rose, violet,* whatever comes to me.

I buy a package of cornbread stuffing from a rock-breasted Mexican granny. Her full-body apron is stamped with red maracas crossed like swords. I'm wagering she put it on so that no minutes would be wasted going from here to home to start cooking. I bet she figured her years of labor were done but now she's raising grandchildren.

She waves goodbye as if she's on a dock and the waters are starting to lift under me.

I feel someone's stare like daggers boring into the back of my neck in the parking lot, and I whirl around: There's no one.

At the neighboring Crossroads World Market, closed for the holiday, I calm myself by peering through the window. Often I'll wander in to inhale the sheer prettiness: Cognac pâté, lupini beans, flans, marzipan hearts. Hayward was once called the Garden of Eden because of the richness of her produce—artichokes, tomatoes, everything. I gave birth to my girls across the township, at Eden Hospital.

At the All-County Building, there's a bronze statue of a crane sprouting branches where a woman sits, her arms stretched upward. A female child with wings flies toward her but is frozen in the pose of not ever getting there. Behind the statue, a bronze older girl faces the opposite direction. She doesn't see the woman or the baby, and nothing of her touches the crane. I used to detour here a lot after my little crack-up teaching literature at Cesar Chávez Middle School. *You're trying to read Yeats to your class, but the kids are pointing their forefingers together, forming the gang-sign "H" for Hayward, like the muzzles of two guns meeting or a goalpost. Students are either doing the H or flicking wadded paper to score goals, and a weight presses your head down until you're gazing at the fortune in shoes: hundred-dollar space-age boots with fluorescent glitter and blinking red blips as if these children have runways on their soles, and your body explodes with flashes; you're like those Japanese kids carted to the hospital when Pokémon cartoons triggered fireworks inside them.*

After Iris McCarthy found me at the DMV and decided I'd ruined her love life, Ric, Joyce, Babette, and Vince told me that angry crackpots come with the territory, and I replied, *No, please, I quit teaching because I want to correct tests that are easy, three choices, pick one, it's right or wrong.* When Iris returned the next day, ranting, Vince, a Vietnam vet, escorted her to the exit and threw her out. He's one of those sweethearts who'd lie down and die for you, and at the same time, as he admits himself, he has absolutely, thoroughly, *given the fuck up.* His grown children are raising their families in Montana, near their mother.

Ric is twenty-four with three infants and has finally stopped asking why I left the classroom. Joyce, our supervisor, calls herself the African Queen and wears huge caftans that force troublemakers to collapse into worship. Babette is gentle and slow, always the one to pad out to Naked Fish Sushi to get the lunch we eat in our cubicles, where we're perched low so that only our heads are visible to the masses huddled in plastic chairs. It's like a bingo parlor: *Now serving B-71 at Window #10! Now serving F-27 at Window #6!* Ric says we look like bobble-heads, and Vince says our skulls are on sticks in a courtyard.

Once I swear Iris slipped into the rest room. No one at the DMV remotely resembles the bathroom signs, a 50s woman in flip hair and tulip skirt, and a man like a manikin from a tuxedo ad. I can't concentrate on that day's count-the-Raiders-wear contest. People are outfitted in silver and black; it's always Raider Nation here. A fellow whose shirt reads "I Live and Die Raiders" hands me his test, and instead of dropping a paper clip into the jar in front of me—the one with the most at 5 o'clock wins $1, the losers chip in a quarter apiece, it's strictly honors system—I'm waiting for Iris to emerge and pierce my heart. The stagecoach on the wall mural flies overhead, over the American Indians happily welcoming settlers to the green shores.

Whenever I drive, I wonder if I'll have to replicate a silly chase scene from one of X's movies.

I round past my old school, over speed bumps decorated with adjoining half-circles, like a toddler's drawing of seagulls. A caped man is the mascot. He rides on the sign that was illuminated until the money ran out. The Lancers.

Yeah, Gina and Blanca used to giggle, *Mami is a Lancer. She's what you do to a boil.*

My house is empty but disheveled; at first I assume Iris has broken in. Gina and Blanca haven't bothered to shut the kitchen drawers spilling out plastic containers. They're smuggling my feast to The Pineapple. The father of my grandbaby, my Annie. I bang open the refrigerator's door: The yam casserole is gouged. The cranberries boiled with ginger are reduced, like a tank with red water stabbed with leaks.

With a vegetable peeler I scrape the strings off some celery for the stuffing, my head bowing toward the drain. *Every car that passes I think is you, coming home.* Why am I bothering? *I dream you up, Lou, Luis, pressing onto me from behind, fitting your head against my shoulder until my face turns to find yours your hands on my breasts Lou the length of you holding my spine in place until my body turns to find you.*

I slam a load of bright colors into the washing machine before I combust with images of The Pineapple gorging on my cooking. Why should Gina and Blanca be kinder to their mother than I was to my own? We lived in a trailer off Hesperian, and when she'd limp home from the sinks where the apricots cooled at Hunts Cannery, she'd stand outside in her housedress, floral, not even with blooms, just sprigs. Did she think my father would abandon his new wife? The torn apron over that dress, flapping in the wind, became the sails of a ghost ship. The cannery closed in the eighties after thriving for a century. One day someone gave us our first washing machine. Mother didn't realize you plug it in. She figured capacity was the thing, you pour in water, pile in the clothes, and your hand fiddles with the propeller in the middle to slosh the water. My friend Beth roared with merriment when she saw Mother washing our clothes like that.

I laughed, too, though I'd been doing the wash the same way. Mother said, "Oh, stars. You mean the machine takes care of me?"

I empty the package of dried cornbread into a basin and soak it with milk.

The girls have no idea about the months I was sure I'd lose their father. He'd come home from Blue Cross and either he was on the verge of an affair or already having one, or maybe he just wanted to be a boy free on a mattress on some floor. Chop a green apple; add garlic, red wine, pecans. Keep going. You can't give up on a holiday. *You live in our house, but you're not here anymore! Look at me! You can't even look at me! At Blue Cross you deal with the histories of ailments, the files groan with them; I'm the one ailing! I'm going to stare into your brown irises and find out if they're holding the film of some woman.*

I grab your collar. My nails dig into your neck, and you seize my wrist. You're twisting away but can't bring yourself to throw me off, and I risk snapping our thread of connection by bleating, Hurry, baby, make love to me, hurry, the girls will be home any minute.

The washing machine shudders to its finish, and I heap the clothes into the basket to tote to the clothesline out back. It's a comfort, fabric tenderized by winter dew, rain. I drop the basket on the patio: Gina has lined the charity cans of food along the fence, like ducks in a shooting gallery.

Mami, don't you know art when you see it?

I hang the clothes, and like many events involving Gina, I can't tell if I'm furious or amused. She likes to shriek, *Fuck this tears-of-a-clown town*, and I echo that, too, but only because I know how gorgeous it is where I've always lived. The Buffalo Bill micro-brewery and antique shops breathe with resurrection, and the Hayward Fishery and Meek Estate, a fairytale castle for ladies' club teas, speak of history, but the beauty I mean is in scouring off the grease—staying—instead of buying new or trusting allure. *Not bolting. Matching the axis of your spine to the pull of the axis in the ground-up earth.* Like when you love someone to pieces and then you and he fall to pieces yourselves and still you love the wreckage—if you stay—as it powders into dust.

As I trap you, you fall backward and crack your head against our framed photo from the Zucchini Festival. You're holding Gina's hand. Blanca's grin reveals missing teeth. We're in front of her third-place-winning entry in the painting contest: A zucchini in a cot dreams himself famous. He's the Mona Lisa as a zucchini; he's a many-angled zuke in a Picasso. You begin lifting your struck head, to take me in.

Goddamn that *slamming door. The girls barrel in,* and Lou and I get put on hold. "So there you are!" I call out.

Gina stomps in, crosses her arms. "If you won't let me invite the father of my child to eat with us, I guess I have to sneak around."

"Oh, by the way, some lady came by, Mami," says Blanca. She's stepped into the line of fire shooting out of my eyes toward Gina.

"A lady?"

"Yeah," says Gina, but she's nervous. "We told her to come back. She said she had a present for you. We thought that sounded good."

I kick the open drawer of plastic containers. The pain travels to jettison out my head to orbit in stars. "I WON'T HAVE IT! I WON'T let some moron you're fucking raise Annie!" I've done it now.

"Annie? Who is Annie, might I ask?" says Gina.

"No one, never mind," I say, and I bark at Blanca to set the table and at Gina to help me truss the turkey. As we both stitch white thread to seal its gaping hole, Gina trills, "Annie banany, where for art thou? Me thinks you rhyme with Granny." Our arms and legs are lifting and falling, and our bodies swaying, and *Lou enters me and without a word he knows I don't want him to move; can we try not to move? Come back to me, my love.* Annie Fanny, sings Blanca, bumping her hip against her sister who returns the dance, and I'm too shy for that but the stars orbiting me melt and drip and *burn into my eyes and finally no one can stay still one inside the other forever, and you lift enough to cover my face with your sweating face while I hold on . . .* Gina caws that she can't open the Kitchen Bouquet to make the gravy, so she's going to run to the Guerrero house to borrow some. "Goodbye, Granny Annie," she says.

"Goodbye, darling."

I tell Blanca to check on the wash and bring in the cans; I could use the olives *but really I must be alone with you and finish how we finished that night. You lifted away still more, and in the very act of drawing back and away, you met my gaze; there was only you and a cloudiness that cleared, letting me see myself sealed upside down in you and* you are back with me for good because it's in my skin how we then rushed away, you ahead of me, lightly on top of the current of sleep.

A crash—Blanca crying, yelling—has me in the back-yard to find Iris waving her silver pistol as if it's glued to her fingers and she's desperate to shake it off. I grab the laundry basket from Blanca and order her inside, but she won't go. I step in front of her, the basket on my hip.

"Iris?" I say. "Put that thing down, and go back home." I have no idea of the make of the gun. I suspect she bought it because she's a woman alone; she follows those urban advice guides. She probably goes from work to gym to nail salon, doing everything she should to prepare for whatever joy is her due but that never arrives because it has nowhere to fit.

From the look of it, she doesn't know how the pistol works.

"Iris, sorry I flunked your test." I used to be a teacher, so I can't stop myself from adding, "Everyone knows that a broken line means you can cross. Not a solid one."

"No," she says. Her gray sweater-dress with its crooked hem looks picked from a catalogue. "A solid line should mean you're solid to cross. Look, I'm not going to hurt you. I just want to shoot this thing for once, practice-like, maybe into that planter over there."

"Come on, will you. Put it on the ground," says Blanca. Her body is wet and vibrating straight through mine.

"You messed up some plans I had, so all I want is to mess up something that's yours," says Iris.

A laugh is a quarter-note, a guffaw is a whole note—and I *guffaw*. "Miss McCarthy, that is *so Hayward* of you. *Look around.* I don't know how much more messed-up anything can get."

Iris stretches the pistol out and away from us, fumbling with the trigger, and without dropping the laundry basket, I grab it from her, and though I've never fired in my life, X suffuses me along with those hours in the dark when he was enormous on screen and hitting his mark, and I am a movie-fed East Bay grease girl from the start, and gripping the silver pistol, I aim at the cans on my fence, and BLAM BLAM BLAM and again BLAM BLAM BLAM, I empty everything out the end of my hand and win the prize on three cans. They've sprung leaks. The noise is stunning. My ears are ringing. I let the basket fall.

"Mami?" Gina has been frozen in the doorframe, holding the Kitchen Bouquet. "Mami, what's this lady doing to you?"

It's just my girl, grown-up and swollen with a baby, out of my flesh and familiar, but Iris is lit with fear: Who's this tough-chick *chola* claiming me as mother? Gina dashes inside, emerges with her handbag, peels some dollar bills off a roll, and lets them drift to the ground. The "DGF" and "XIV" have been washed down to faint stains on her knuckles. Iris takes a step back. "We always pay for the bullets for our target practice," Gina says. She confiscates the pistol from the lock of my fist.

Iris is quaking. Her razor-cut hair is sprayed into immobility. I pick up the money and cram it into her hand, and she trips in her hurry out the back gate.

Gina props up one side of Blanca and I take her on the other as we steer her inside on her wobbling pins. The photo of us now fits watery but tight as a contact lens over the episode at Sulfur Creek at a children's party sponsored by H.A.R.D., the Hayward Area Recreational District, when Blanca sobbed at how her friends were lashing the kangaroo piñata . . . her first proof that children will pummel anything sweet into a road-kill nightmare. Gina held her arm then, too, waiting for me, not afraid to claim timid Blanca as her own. Planted next to my ancient mother while my friend Beth is laughing, I picture watching as Gina pitches a dime onto the floor and snarls,

Here's what I owe for the Pepsi you bought, now get out. It's washday the way we know it in the house where I live.

We'll have to deal with the police, surrender the pistol, and file a report. Iris might get put away for a while, and then she'll vanish, or grow crazier, or come back. There's no such thing as an Eden that's not banged-up.

Up the street in Fairview, there's a vista where San Francisco gleams like a halved geode, too expensive, an Emerald City, too far, and yet it feels like mine. Here right now with me there's a dot of desire inside Annie that's my great-grandchild. I give it a year or two before Gina will be pounding down the door, wailing that The Pineapple is bored and the baby won't quit squalling. *Stay with me,* I'll say, and then she'll be gone again. And when the days go on and on, out of the blue will come flowers that tell me it is good to see moments only as snapshots with their edges bleeding and then to let them go.

Our centerpiece is the vase of gladioli and the pipe-cleaner turkey that my mother and I twisted back when everyone's dad smoked a pipe and children learned to make giraffes and creatures from the bristly cleaning wires. One fabulous year, the pipe-cleaner people produced them in color. The girls taunt my scrawny pipe-cleaner turkey. We have our annual traditions to uphold.

Blanca insists she can perform the carving. Gina holds the huge fork with tines blackened from the time she was six and used it to roast her shoe in the fireplace, because she wanted to run away from home and was practicing being a hobo. Blanca's hand shakes; she giggles as the leg resists the knife. She nicks the torso as if she's torturing it.

Our bronzed bird sprouts branches and I'm sitting on them and the winged child is within reach.

Gina yells, "You dumb ass, you don't have to kill it anymore!" She stabs the fork deep into the breast. I've heard that turkeys will throw back their heads in a rainstorm and drown. It's as good a stupid way to die as any. I'm mighty with sadness. I've always been fevered with love to bursting, but love could very well be done for me.

Ah but here's a moment for you. My girls turn to me with mouths open and stop—a dead full halt—as the bird runs and runs with fluid, grease like a river, and—this will be our grace tonight—Gina says astonished, scarcely breathing, "Look at this, Mami. What did you do to get it so tender?"

the rice artist

the explosion blew up Angelo's daughter. a crazy teacher had planted the bomb. no bodies existed for burial. Karen and the other little ones were atomized.

Angelo looked for her on the vibrissae inside nostrils. strong winds might carry her to plug a limpet's hole. was she that sparkle on the eyelashes of that woman in love? she landed like spice on the tops of coffees in the café, this child who'd sung to cats and who'd written, "I want to be a spy when I grow up."

using his magnifying glass and a stiff thread dipped in ink, he fit the Our Father onto a grain of rice. another grain was the Hail Mary; another, the Glory Be. when he ran out of prayers, he marked a sack of rice with *Paradise Lost*.

his wife, Eliza, flew sideways out of the house. she sent him a postcard from a bar in Texas. a blank card from St. Louis. he'd watched her sail off as if she were a bride in a painting by Chagall, though instead of her hair being wild from nights of love it was tangled as if she'd been rolling in a forest.

trucks rumbled past his house, carrying spare, Swedish furniture, disturbing him.

he moved to the shore, but crickets sawed their legs.

roses screamed with the sex life of bees.

he moved inland, and a yogi taught him to control his nerves and the flow of his blood. he stopped feeling his skin. his fingers, once the size of piano keys, shrank into paper swathing skeleton. his testicles dried until the veins appeared dabbed on like the lines on the lips of orchids.

he carved specks of sawdust into dogs, cats, and owls. he used a high-power magnifier to create witches out of sugar grains, cutting only in the second and a half between his heartbeats. a comb's teeth offered crevices to trap a platoon of witches. each carving took three months. women in cocktail dresses he set in the eyes of needles. an espionage agent rested on a match's head. he could work between his heartbeats for thirty hours without stopping, and often the yogi needed to pry Angelo's fingers apart, because his nerves, laboring so closely, stuck together.

his crowning work was to carve angels out of sawdust. one angel he set on the head of a pin, and two angels danced on her head, and three on each of their heads, until he had not only a spray of angels but, in his miniature way, the answer to that old riddle: an infinity of angels can dance . . . but infinity has gotten away with murder by refusing to be reducible and countable. dozens of angels made of dust are as valiant as infinity—more, since they offer their tender, minute bodies for a counting that so sadly falls short. the angels took three years to finish.

New York: *I've met someone new*, read Eliza's postcard.

at a gallery displaying his angels, rice, secret agents, witches, and animals, he did not hear the cries of amazement as the crowd surged from one glass globe to the next; everyone was forced to stop and bend down to be shocked by the magnifications. at the opening, he spied a woman with the haunches of a panther, and the gold off the overhead lights fit coins over her eyes. a spume of champagne fizzed on her lip.

Angelo was alert to distant noises when he took her behind the gallery, but no one was anywhere to be seen, and, absent from his own show, he kissed the woman madly and when she said, enter me & stay there, he did, his heartbeats going mad, all training lost, and when he exploded he did not mind having gone to so much care, all for an uncontrollable flinging of his limbs, a moan he failed to swallow, a sensation of other skin ripping through him so it might well kill him, all so he might go back as if forever to the beginning of his time.

- desire + loss of innocence

Fig. 3 (BACK). *I asked love to sweep me away, but it galloped ahead of me.*

The Glass Eaters

I was my mother's mother until I turned sixteen. She was in love for years with a married man named Frank Connelly, and it took all she had to hold down a job at a caterer's in town. She would stand for a moment bracing herself in our open doorway when she arrived home from work, exhausted, still wearing her apron, as if she had managed a violent escape from an Edward Hopper painting.

I always helped her out of her kitchen whites and steadied her into the hot water I ran in the bathtub, where her fair skin immediately flamed to rose. I washed off her nightly seal of grease, and then she liked a bristle brush to scour her skin. She was thin, but in my arms she seemed to go lighter—and then lighter still, to a kind of floating that would scare most children but not me, because I understood that she wanted to bathe away her flesh to get to the burning inside her, that fierce but weightless burning. A coral-colored birthmark was on her flat stomach, and I imagined Frank kissing it. I was a happy but fearful guardian and did not want an excess of waiting to kill her.

The Love Life of an Assistant Animator

We were renting a little white stucco house with a terra-cotta roof, hemmed in with cyclone fencing, on C Street in the old part of Hayward. I had almost no memory of my father, James Duarte, who left when I was five. He called from Florida twice a year, on my birthday and at Christmas, his voice furtive and hasty, as if he were in the Federal Witness Protection program. I suspect he was a pleasant, normal man, decent and bewildered. I own one photo of him, faded the way snapshots from the sixties become, as if developed not with chemicals but with honey. He is holding my hand at Bolinas Beach, where I learned that agates lose their sheen out of water.

My mother and I had a view of the Hayward hills but not of San Francisco's silver skyline, like a stilled wind chime, west across the Bay, where Frank lived and worked. He was what is now called an old-fashioned lawyer, with a battered Toyota and a heavy docket of pro-bono cases. I was eleven when he entered our lives and my career as my mother's mother began, but the odd thing was that up until I was sixteen, when everything turned upside down, I never actually met him. My mother was secretive, a lovesick teenager; I could not convince her not to be ashamed. They made their arrangements on the phone late at night. Occasionally I caught a glimpse of Frank when he dropped her off, as I was pacing the floor and peering through the curtains. My friend Lacey once asked how I could stand my mother having nothing left for me, but that was never how I felt. On the days she was to see Frank, and for a full day afterward, she gave off more joy than anyone I have ever come to know.

I was a cheerful, terrible housekeeper. My mother's yellow hair and my black strands skittered over the floorboards, loosely braiding lightness and darkness. I let Mama drop her clothes on the floor, and it would be days before I picked them up. For a long time, I thought washing dishes was like washing underwear, that people used one item after another and cleaned the heap when the supply ran out. On Sundays, I aimed our Impala like a gunboat down Jackson Street to buy groceries at Lucky's. I usually cooked what I think of now as a child's party menu: lots of tomato soup and cheddar on Roman Meal bread. I had been driving since thirteen, the moment I was a head above the wheel, and Mama never objected. It never occurred to me that Lacey was right when she said that I needed a license.

I often insisted that Mama come to Lucky's with me, where she gazed at women with men—not with jealousy, but with amazement. How could they be content with someone who was not Frank? She had none of the giddy illusion that most of us have in a store, that everything on display is ours for the taking. What can be done with a child single-hearted in her obsessions? My mother lacked all drive toward beautiful strangers.

The disruption started when Frank became famous. He prosecuted a refinery for allowing solvents to seep into the water table, and it was enough of a David-versus-Goliath victory for him to make the circuit of environmental fundraisers, dinners, and conventions. Then came a book contract and trips to Sacramento to read his opinion into various records.

The first casualty in Frank's life was that he moved out of the house he shared with his wife. "Isn't that fabulous, Julia?" my mother said to me sharply one evening at dinnertime, after Frank called to say he could not see her that night. "He is now *sep-are-rated*."

"That's good, isn't it?"

"Good! Yes indeed. Separated," she said, not to me, but toward some tribunal only she could see in the air. "Then there's *divorce*, and *recovery* from divorce, and then—what?"

"I don't know, Mama. Time for him to start out with you."

"Start? We're starting? Let's see. Then there's the period with some other woman so your best beloved isn't the one *burdened* with you after the divorce, and there's the recovery from *that*—"

I had read *Great Expectations* in English class and had long been on the watch against her veering from exalted anticipation toward the realm of waiting—waiting much, much too long—in the style of Miss Havisham. Now I saw that my mother feared the same thing.

And then one night, Frank stood her up. That had never happened before, and it ruined the pleasure I took in helping her get ready. Lacey and I loved going to Capwell's to collect the sampler vials of perfumes so that I could dab Chanel No. 5 or Opium at my mother's pulse points. I would help her choose a lace shift, or a sea-pattern scarf for her blue dress, pretending I did not know why she was leaving the house. She never saw Frank when she was not resplendent—bathed and powdered, eyebrows penciled, earrings glistening.

She called his new apartment twice, but there was no answer. At last she took off her dress with its embroidered bolero jacket and rolled down her black stockings. She undid her silver hair clip and put on her robe and sank into the chair in our living room, the one with the gold threads sticking out like broken guitar strings.

"I'm going to set your hair for you, Mama," I said. "Won't that be nice?" She seemed not to hear me. I set out a glass of water, dipped a comb in it, and curled pinches of her hair around my finger and fixed them to her head with Xs of bobby pins. The idea was to get a ballet or flamenco dancer's sharp, flat hook at both cheeks.

"Don't be sad, Mama," I said.

"I'm not. I'm tired."

I turned on the television—and there was Frank, being interviewed about the refinery case. My mother did something that struck us both, instantly, as strange: Her hands flew to her hair, clamped down with artillery. She clutched her stained robe, as if Frank were looking at her. It was the first time she had not been perfectly lovely in his presence. She and I looked at each other and laughed. I stared back at the set, thinking, there's my mother's lover in a suit and tie. I am setting the hair of someone who has seen that handsome man naked. It absolutely electrified me.

"See?" I said. "He probably hasn't had time to call."

"I would like him to see me as I am right now," said my mother. "It's time for that, don't you think?" She stopped trying to hide herself with her hands. She said that ordinary life could be about love, with its daily erosions and unguarded moments; didn't I think so?

I looked at her uneasily and said sure. That was love, too.

She was from the generation of women who kept Kleenex tucked into the wrists or pockets of their clothing—sad, lumpy corsages, as if they were grimly practical about the eventuality of tears, and she extracted some tissue from her robe and began to cry.

I would do anything never to hear again the weeping that came from my mother that night. I got up three times to go quiet her. She was frightened by noises after dark, by the mating call of cats, like a baby's crying; possums and raccoons put her in mind of thieves. Hayward was good-sized, with streets like Mission Boulevard, and car dealerships, Val's Burgers, and the Hayward Plunge swimming arena—where did these animals sleep during daylight? When Frank left his wife, it lifted my mother's hopes out of waiting into possibility; it was excruciating to be asked to find a last reserve of patience.

She stopped picking up the phone, and the answering machine filled our house with Frank's haunting voice, "Clarissa? Clarissa? Are you there? Darling, please." Without telling me where she was going, she struck out on walks and was feverish when she came home. I would control my temper as I sat her down, felt her forehead, and said, "Now, what do you mean by running off like that?"

"Oh—as if I had anywhere to go!"

"You should call Frank. What's the matter with you?"

"With me? There's nothing at all the matter with *me*."

"You're burning up."

Contact with her was conducting a jolt into my nerves. I'd had a bout of fibrillations when I was fourteen, and a doctor told me that I had "a fullness of heart." I had not fathomed, until now, what he meant: I was to inherit my mother's fever. My campaign with boys was relentless. All I had to do for them to make love to me was look directly into their eyes. The hours when I could not vent my desire were exercises in empty time. The fascinating part was afterward, after something fast in a car or in some corner of the Knowland Park Zoo; they would not meet my gaze, as if they had never met me.

The cure for the awful pang this gave me, I soon discovered, was to find someone else as soon as possible. Why should I suffer as my mother did, weighing myself down with a single choice that the world was determined to deny me? I never abandoned the care of my mother, but every now and then I was not there when she came home, or she was not there when I returned, and I had no idea if she were seeing Frank again or going on her crazy walks. Lacey said, "God, you're like a man, Julia. Or Catherine the Great. She'd wander through her regiments and say, 'You tonight. You tomorrow.'"

The first boy I was sorry to leave was Leon, a cross-country runner with parents from the Dominican Republic who came to sit in the stands to watch him dash out of sight, which was more than I managed for him. They stood to applaud as the team no one cared about vanished from Hayward High's playing field. When I told Leon I figured we were through, his face was like a stone thing with a face inside it. We had made love twice in his baby-blue Chevrolet, and once the impression of his name on his letterman's jacket had pressed itself on my bare breast before disappearing. And for a moment, I wondered: How did the foot on the sewing machine know how to make the loops in the shape of his name? He remarked that his parents would adore me—thanks to my missing father, I was half-Latina—and then he blurted that they would be equally fond of my Irish-and-Dutch mother. Ireland and Holland also had fine civilizations.

He kept following me, staring. He did not know the rule that now he was supposed to pretend not to know me. I said that he had to stop, and he insisted on buying dinner for me at the Hick'ry Pit. No other boy had asked me for an actual date. Pigs in chef's toques and aprons were painted on the walls, waving tongs and spatulas. We ordered our barbecue, but other than that we did not speak until I asked Leon, "Are you sad because you miss me?"

"No," he said. "You're short. Black straight hair is for witches. You're ugly. Your eyes are the color of people who get seasick, and your skin is so white I'd think you'd seen a ghost—if you had any conscience about seeing anything but yourself." He pulled a strip of red meat off a sparerib with his teeth.

"You think I'm ugly?"

He dropped the bone onto his plate and gasped, reining in a sob. "No," he said.

I burst into tears. "Oh, Leon. I'm so sorry."

He reached across the table and held my hand and asked if I would consider marrying him when we graduated from high school.

"I can't, Leon," I said. "I don't know you, and you don't know me."

"How long do I have to know you?" he said.

I was silent.

"All right, then," he said quietly. He drove me home, kissed my forehead, and we never spoke again.

My mother had been waiting up for me.

I had often thought she could smell love on my skin, but this time I must have given off the scent of having hurt someone. When I stepped through the front doorway, she slapped me hard. Something had changed; she had decided to be my mother once again, and I did not like this, not one bit.

She was immobile, reading an article in *Gracious Living* magazine. It was about the ice sculptor Yukio Matsuo, and the title was "A Rodin of the North Pole." She was holding the magazine in front of her the way choirboys on Christmas cards hold out sheets of music. There was a photo of a flying fish carved from ice called "Joyful Summer," and one of several waves, back-lit with pastel blues, called "Tsunami." I had to admit that freezing a powerful surge of emotion—in both examples—was breathtaking. How had he managed to carve flight, actual flight, into blocks of ice?

Mama had studied ice carving years before at the Culinary Institute in San Francisco, when I was too small to remember much. I knew that she was good at *garde-manger* and could pour a *chaud-froid* over salmon, but her nine-to-five shift at Estrela's Catering gave her little chance for anything beyond producing trays of sliced meats and pineapple boats for office parties.

Her boss Gary, though, said she was welcome to stay late at the kitchen, use the walk-in freezer, and carve ice to her heart's content—mermaids, ships, seahorses. Gary was sweet on my mother, realized he didn't have a chance, and was gentle in his disappointment. One night when I was there, begging her to come home, she was alone but buoyant in the cold industrial kitchen, with its stainless-steel tables that looked as if they belonged in an animal hospital. She showed me how to run a saw over one surface of a block of ice, then turn the blade over and re-score the same plane. She did the same to another plane on another block. "Turning a saw" would allow the blocks to be joined, because the metal generated enough disturbance and warmth to seal the ice together without a seam. Where had her energy come from?

She was busy; Frank was busy. He was finishing a lecture tour in the Northwest, but he promised my mother that he would do his best to come back a few days early, because he missed her. He had agreed that the time had come to meet me and for the two of them to go, as he put it, "public."

On the night he was due to fly in and drive to Hayward, I was nervous. I put on a long velvet skirt and lace blouse with a cameo, the sort of outfit that chaste girls wear in clothing catalogues at holiday time. I passed a cloth over most of the surfaces of the house and vacuumed the hardwood floor and told my mother to wear crystal earrings with her black dress. We needed to keep it simple. The main attraction that night should not be us, but the ice sculpture she had brought home to show him, her first unveiling.

It was called *Glass Within Glass*. A cry had caught in my throat when she pulled away the aluminum wrapping. I had no idea my mother could do anything so marvelous. A real wineglass was imbedded within a block carved in the shape of a glass. The idea was to have an event that lasted long enough for the ice-goblet to melt away and offer the genuine glass, brilliantly chilled, and a couple could toast the end of their evening. She set it on a tray on our dining-room table, under the wrought-iron chandelier. She had replaced the plain bulbs with blue ones.

"Mama," I said, and then I could not speak.

"Shall I tell you how I did it?" She put an arm around me and kissed the top of my head.

"No," I said. "No, please don't." That would be like a magician revealing his secrets. I could guess: She had filled a mold halfway with water, frozen it, and put a glass on the frozen ledge. Then she had filled the rest of the block, frozen everything, and carved the goblet shape with the glass locked inside. That would be the difficult part for people to figure out—the patience required for that second stage of freezing.

My mother and I waited for Frank in our small living room. We hardly moved or talked: *Duartes Within Home* and *Glass Within Glass*. At ten o'clock, we shared the merlot we had been saving. The room grew chilly, but the ice kept melting under the lights. When I told her that I was sad to watch it vanishing, she said no, that was the strength of ice sculpture. Its mystery was in how its beauty unfolded, moment by moment, showing a good silhouette even while it was dissolving. This, too, should be seen as perfect, though not new or pristine, even as the evening stretched on and finally ended. I had to agree with her, as the wineglass appeared, lip first, then body. Ice goes whiter as it melts, as if in its dying it finds its most intense color. And the blue of the lights played here and there as the ice changed. We chipped away what remained and freed the glass at eleven at night, and her earrings refracted beams. We stood for a while: *Duarte Women at Close of Day*. The phone rang. My mother stayed motionless.

"Are you going to answer it, or shall I?" I said.

"Eleven o'clock, Julia. That's why we have the expression, Eleventh Hour. As in, 'He didn't show up until the eleventh hour.'"

Frank had missed a connection and was still in Seattle, but he would soon, he promised, be home for us both. Time and schedules often refused to cooperate, said my mother, with the best of plans.

Frank caught me entirely by surprise. My hair was bound up in a bandana as I repainted our porch; over the years, the red surface had blistered to impetigo. It was a Saturday, and my mother was practicing her ice-work at the caterer's on her day off. The bucket of paint was next to me inside the house, where I was kneeling to finish the last brush-strokes, when a tall man with thick hair and an armful of roses came up the walkway and said, "You must be Julia."

"Hello, Frank, welcome to Versailles," I said, still crouching in the doorway. "What brings you to the greasy side of the Bay?" This was not fair, but I was embarrassed at how I looked.

"May I came in?" he said.

We looked down at the porch and laughed. When I stood, he tossed the roses for me to catch and said, "And now me." I set the roses down and held out my hands, reaching over the wet paint, and he hoisted himself over my work and into the house, tripping forward into my grasp, where he stayed a moment to hug me and say, "I'm glad to meet you." His sights roamed the living room, and when I said it wasn't much, he said no, it was wonderful, it was everything. He wanted me to take him at once to my mother, wherever she was. I warned that she was in a bad mood since he had been stuck in Seattle. He said he understood. That was why he was now here.

She did not bother to look up when Frank and I entered Estrela's Catering. Gary and two of the cooks were relieved to see us. My mother was running a steel tool across a block of ice as if she were shaving the head of a recruit. She landed a hammer on a corner, and ice sprayed into the air.

"Clarissa?" said Frank. "What are you doing, dear?"

Whack! She took a minute to enjoy a rich, inner joke.

"Well, Frank, if you'd been here all along, there'd be no need for me to explain anything, would there."

"I don't know about that, Clarissa. People need things explained even when they know each other pretty well."

"Is that so." Crack!

"Look. How about if I get you out of here? You and Julia and I can go out to dinner."

"That's a terrific idea," I said. "Isn't it, Mama?"

Gary said, "Everything okay over there?" He had a gaunt, stringy aspect; life was toughening him in fairly useless ways.

"I think we're fine here, Gary, thanks," said Frank.

"I like it here. I spend a lot of time here, Frank, the way you do in Seattle and San Francisco and wherever else your charm calls you," said my mother. "Gary is quite a decent boss."

Gary sank a bit—a good fellow once again, but nothing more.

"And I spend a lot of time in my office, Lissy. I don't bore you with a play-by-play because not much of it's interesting," said Frank.

"That's a pity. I find what I'm doing very interesting."

"Not every moment."

"Every moment."

Frank lowered his voice. "Clarissa. We're going to be together soon. We're together right now, as far as I can see. That's what counts. Doesn't it? Why are you wasting time with things that melt?"

A fury passed over her before she held up the chisel. "Do you know what this is, Frank?"

"A weapon."

"A gouge chisel. Good for details. Fish fins. A flower."

I don't know why she had assumed the tone of a docent in an Ice Sculpture Museum (where presumably the replicas would be in glass).

"I'm sure of it, dear," said Frank. "Shall I take you somewhere?"

"The *point* is the melting. 'Subzero Art.' A celebration, you might say, of nothing lasting, because what else can people do? *The Last Supper* was painted and left to fade in a dining hall, I believe. Some people might say that's not very smart."

Frank leaned down and took my mother's face in his hands and kissed her. They stayed in a kiss, and Gary turned away, and so did I, unaccustomed to their private life on display. My mother was pretty, but an abundance of pretty women lived in San Francisco, and sometimes I wondered what Frank saw in her. Now I knew: He thrived on his fights with the world, but she had the artist's view that drive and creation could make what was unimportant in the world drop away. I remembered when she would float in my arms as I bathed her, when she was predicting for me that one day all but the strong, mysterious light in her would perish. This perishing was a simple fact of living, and she did not fear it, and what a pity that most people never surrendered their strength in order to summon up such a blessing, such a light.

Frank arranged for my mother to present an ice sculpture at a cocktail party to be held at the State Capitol. The Capitol's facilities would provide drinks and a cake, and my mother could display her work on an adjoining table. Details of the event remained vague. Certain environmental bills were about to clear the Senate, and he was being asked to offer a few uplifting words about the waterways of California. The party would be in the Columbus Rotunda, where Colombo wears brocade clothes and holds a map, all of it marble; the carver had found softness in the white stone. This statue had been a highlight during an eighth-grade field trip, to illustrate that a famous voyager had once been a child like us.

My mother was thrilled at what she called her "coming-out party" and decided to copy the Matsuo work called *Endeavor*. A fish is perched evenly on a level platform. Behind it is a smaller fish on a lower platform that tilts, as if yearning, toward the first, grander one. My mother thought it would be an homage to everyone striving to guard water life. Gary loaned us the truck with the freezer unit, and Frank agreed to drive it.

He was at the wheel with my mother beside him, her arm along the back of the driver's seat—a classic pose of workaday affection. We took the 580 to the 680, past the scars freshly cut for new housing developments in the Concord hills. Just as my mother was about to lean her head onto his shoulder, Frank shifted, and I knew he was deciding whether to voice a reality that I was also sensing: Something was burning. A faint smell was rising out of the back of the truck.

"We'd better stop," he said. My mother sat up and looked at him with alarm.

"What do you mean?" she said.

"I think the coils are short-circuiting," he said.

"No," said my mother. "No."

"Haven't you been smelling something funny?" I said.

"No," said my mother. "I haven't."

We continued our enactment of the classic Dad-in-action—the suburban version of re-lashing the ties to the mast—as Frank pulled the truck over and got out to investigate. Cars hurled past as he opened the latch to the back door and rattled around inside. My mother did not turn around to look at me until Frank returned to the driver's seat.

We merged onto the freeway and drove under a few highway signs before my mother said, "For God's sake, Frank. Tell me what's wrong."

He shrugged. "The coils are burned out. One might still be working. We'll get there in half an hour and find a freezer. If the event starts on time, maybe a little late, we'll be fine."

We stared ahead in silence. The traffic snarled as we hit the curveball glide where the 80 stretches out of the 680 toward Sacramento, through Vacaville, Fairfield, and Dixon, with their signs for pistachios, artichokes, and strawberries. The tomatoes that had flown off shipping trucks put red smears on the roadway, like mouths without their faces rising from somewhere deep inside the asphalt.

"Well, it's not your fault, is it," said my mother.

"No," he said. "It isn't. It isn't Gary's fault either."

"That I don't know about," said my mother.

"I do," said Frank.

"We're almost there," I said.

He knew the Capitol but not the location of the service entrance. It took us a while to find it. A madman was shouting from a staircase, calling over the trim, colorful flowerbed meant to enthrall visitors with the state's native beauty. Squirrels raced on the lawn as if trying to herd the sightseers. The heat was thoroughly defeating, and heavy people wandered around as if turning on a rotisserie. I could see the meat falling off everyone's bones.

A sheet of water poured over the front of my mother as she and Frank lifted the covered sculpture from the back of the truck. "Damn it," she said. "Oh, what have I got us into?"

"You're fine," said Frank. "We're all of us fine."

"You've done great, Mama," I said.

But the tray was heavy, and we staggered carrying it down some stairs to a kitchen where we were met by a sour woman who informed us that storing ice in her freezer was out of the question.

"It isn't ice, Ma'am. It's the main event," said Frank.

The woman replied, her register becoming vivid, that there was no room for any main events in her deep freeze. Service people in black trousers, white shirts, and black bow ties observed us. They were setting up tables with white tablecloths and glasses and bottles in the adjacent rotunda. A plain sheet cake was near the wine. A man who saw our plight tilted his head toward a spare side table, and we set Mama's ice sculpture there and pulled off the wrapping.

Endeavor was in bad shape. The smaller, striving fish was an hour away from being a complete abstraction, reduced to something that looked like an anvil. The larger fish was dripping water from its barbels. The definition was gone from its fins. I said something earnest and stupid about *Endeavor* now being closer to *Accomplishment*, because the smaller fish was merging with the larger one.

My mother, her front soaking wet, glared at me with the contempt of a child who has heard too many lies from an imaginative adult.

"Sweetheart," said Frank. My mother was shaking, and he sat her down on the ledge near Colombo. The low-ceilinged mural showed ships arriving in the New World, with the legend, "The Work of Man Is Incomplete." I suggested we go for a walk and see the statue of Isabella, the trompe l'oeil lions, the carved staircases.

My mother buried her face in her hands and moaned softly. Frank put his arm around her.

"We could go see the shadow-boxes of the counties," I said.

"Lassen's is the best," Frank said to me. Lassen's box was labeled "Untouched Beauty" and showed a boy scaling rocks and a man fishing.

I said I liked Technicolor Orange County. They had rigged up whirligig Disneyland things, and Solano County was good, with its cutouts of milk farms and—what cheer in their daily lives!—a cow jumping over the moon. Frank agreed that Solano's was fantastic.

"You can tell which counties slopped something together, and which ones did their homework and made a nice box-art display," said Frank. He gave my mother a hug. "Tell you what, Clarissa. It's time for me to go throw my speech at them, but I'll cut it in half and tell them the wine supply is running low in the rotunda and they'd better get here fast. I'll be back as soon as I can." He kissed her again and said, "As soon as I can."

The moments when I was alone with my mother, her face still stuck in her hands, seemed endless and horrifying, but it wasn't really long before Frank returned, ashen. His words of uplift had been drowned out by what was transpiring on the Senate floor—a screaming match about who was responsible for the fish in Lake Stanislaus being dead. The Fish and Game people had said, We need to dump magic poison into the lake to kill off only the pike, because they're killing off the nice fish, the sportsmen's fish. And the environmental people had said, No, no, you can't. The Fish and Game people had said, We can, and here's the paper to prove it, and they dumped the magic poison into Lake Stanislaus. And it killed the pike and hundreds—thousands?—of the nice fish, their bellies exploding and releasing a fresh shock of magic poison for the pike and nice fish that had missed it the first time. And the environmental guys were screeching, and the Fish agency was yelling, The magic poison has never failed, and you people are always calling us and saying, Do something! The sportsmen have stopped coming here! Our children are going to starve!

My mother looked at him, stood, and said, "What?"

Our heads turned slowly toward her dripping statue. So did the heads of the service people setting out the glasses.

"Oh, God," I said.

"They'll think I'm laughing at them," said my mother. "They'll all think I'm laughing at them!"

"You could throw it out," said Frank. "No one will be the wiser."

"I could what?" My mother's face tightened.

"Mama," I said. "He's not saying it isn't good, he's just saying right here for right now, fish that seem to be dying might be a bad idea."

"That's all I meant, Clarissa," said Frank. "It's up to you. Darling, don't deliberately misunderstand what I said."

"I'm happy to let everyone laugh at me," she said.

"I'm not," said Frank.

"Then you'll have to tell them to stop, maybe, Frank. How about that?"

While the two of them stood lock-still, staring at each other, with me chiming in that Frank was only trying to protect her, the crowd roared in and headed for the bar. Hardly anyone noticed my mother's ice sculpture at all. That was the simple truth of it. They were arguing about the dead fish in Lake Stanislaus, and Frank got swept up in the crowd and carried away from us. My mother and I hovered near the table with *Endeavor* and watched Frank work the room. He was good at it. I studied how he knew when to move his head enough to get away from a bore. Women liked him and stood close to him when they talked.

A few people saw my mother's damp clothing and said, "You been swimming in the poisoned lake?" One or two glanced at the sculpture after collecting their drinks. A top dorsal fin was tilted forward and still seemed to be waving, moving fast through water, but it was getting harder to tell what this thing was.

A large blond woman, drunk, leaned toward the ice fish and said merrily, "Well, that has seen better days." White wine from her plastic cup sloshed onto the table.

"So have you," I said.

I thought she might throw her wine in my face. Instead, she drained her plastic glass and tossed it as a parting gesture at the ice.

"Very nice," I said, knocking the glass to the floor.

"I am a woman of long afternoons," said my mother, "and this is one of the longest."

"Does it bother you that women are all over Frank?" I asked.

She said no, she loved his ease in moving through the world. It confirmed her faith in humanity that everyone would find him pleasing.

"Well, I've had enough now," I said. "More than enough."

I found Frank listening to a woman describing her trip to Barcelona. There was a plaza in the heart of the city where young men and women, desperate, would smash and eat glass. Blood would pour from their cut mouths. Tourists would throw money and scream at them to stop, but the more money thrown the more glass would be chewed, and it got to such a fever pitch of glass and people tossing spare change, the woman said, that she avoided the plaza altogether. But even now she could not get this spectacle out of her mind. All that need and want, and addiction—so raw! So public!

I pulled Frank's sleeve. I looked at the woman and said, "Maybe you should have gone up to them and said, Tell me how much it takes for you to stop hurting yourself, and I'll give it to you. Whatever you need."

Frank said, "Excuse me," to both of us. He said, Excuse me, excuse me, pardon me, please, let me through, until he was across the room where my mother stood, shivering and wet, her work pouring in streams off the table.

85

My mother met Frank at a "happening," a sound-bathing program at the art-deco Paramount Theater in Oakland. The sounds filling the auditorium began with the realistic—"Church Bells," "Train Whistle"—and moved to the abstract: "Awe," "Anguish." She instinctively grabbed his hand during the real—at "Water"—because he was sitting alone next to her. That was when happiness began for me, too, when I was fated to undertake the care of my mother, when she had nothing to spare but I did, when Frank returned her grasp and did not let go.

Much of the pleasure must have been in how unambiguous, how clarified each moment was for the audience. Because what real moment in a real life is not wracked with dozens of contradictions, each of them true? Frank was embarrassed by my mother's work; Frank was of course not embarrassed by my mother's work and wanted to shield her from harm. My mother's pride was hurt; my mother was choosing to be misunderstood. Each moment passes, to allow for the complexities of the next, already complicated by what has preceded.

Frank told my mother he would love her forever, and that was true. And then his days after the party at the Capitol settled back into a hectic pace. He swore this would be temporary—and no doubt this also could have been true, quite so, but the speed with which my mother reacted was breathtaking.

She decided we would leave our rented house in Hayward and try our luck in Chicago, where we knew no one. She was hired as a *sous*-chef in a hotel that allowed her to do an occasional ice sculpture for banquets. Two years later, when I was leaving to attend the Art College of Design in Pasadena, Frank arrived in Chicago. He had come to see her; he had come to ask if he might stay.

During my brief career as a wild girl in high school, I attended (the compensatory drive) some catechism classes. I no longer recall why I nursed the fantasy that my mother and I should attend Easter Mass. The richest part of that fruity charade would be at the time for communion, forbidden to us both—the unrepentant mistress of a married man and the girl who was letting boys jump onto her skeleton as if they were putting out a fire.

I do remember Sister Margarida's description of eternity: Imagine that a bird carries a grain of sand and drops it. The bird waits a million years, then gets another grain to drop onto the first one. Then a million years pass again before the bird goes after the third grain.

Now imagine that the bird has to build one million mountains each consisting of one million grains of sand. What is that—even that!—compared to eternity? Consider this before committing a sin that will send you to everlasting flames!

But what if each of those grains is a life, full of what some people call sin and what others will call episodes of living? What if you swallow that sin or life instead of dropping it? What if you keep it in your belly a million years before you go find it again—and it was joy, so you fly much faster than you should, and so you bring together fire and flight, and sand—and that, as I understand it, creates glass; heat that brings sand to explosion. We would form a seasoned flock of glass birds, with eternity spinning inside us, preserved in our burning.

Frank Connelly and my mother were married for ten years and then divorced. This is the constant human experiment—to try, in the face of all evidence, to make both ravishing and ordinary love deepen in a marriage. Frank moved to New York. I believe he remarried, but my mother did not. I saw him one last time, a long while later, when my mother was dying of breast cancer at age fifty-nine in a Chicago hospital.

I met Frank in the hospital's lobby, where we embraced. His hair had whitened and receded.

I led him to her room. He stopped and could not take his eyes off her. "Isn't she beautiful?" he said.

She was wan but beaming and held out her arms.

"You've kept me waiting," she said—and there it was, then as always, continuing, the story of their lives. Even this was within the spell of their passion: to be apart long enough to ensure that the end would be just like this, just like their beginning.

Scalings

Which unhappiness will it be? wondered Dorothea, waiting on the upstairs divan. Picking at a gold loop loose in the furniture, she practiced sitting as she would on the train, insouciant (a word a friend had recently taught her). When a fellow passenger offered to buy her a crème de menthe in the dining car—no, a Bloody Mary, crème de menthe belonged with pineapple and ice cream for children—she would say, "Why, how kind! We're several drinks from Chicago, true?" He—Luc, something French—would mention being in the assaying business. She would picture him putting the treasure of a customer in one pan and lead bars in the opposing scale to determine the weight. Dorothea smoothed her coral-colored skirt. She had a handkerchief soaked in lavender water, a beige blouse (plain pressed white was for schoolgirls), and textured stockings; what else should accent her journey? Did women go toward their new lives wearing hats these days? She tried not to resent her mother getting married so old; Mother believed in hats, but who could trust her ideas to be young?

It will come at any moment, the cry. The cry when Mother finds her antique locket missing. It cannot be a goodbye present, because Dorothea had sold it to get out of South Bend in the first place. Sitting here was a necessary charade. What an awful unhappiness, if Mother suspected . . . impossible, Dorothea couldn't let herself worry about that now. More likely Mother would assume that when cousin Lettie visited last week with her five children, they made off with not only those few pieces of silver and the chocolate rabbit and the Wedgwood creamer, but with the locket, whose emerald was an unblinking green eye. Mother always said that Lettie's stealing from them was right with God; she would never accuse her, poor Lettie, stuck alone with so many kids. At least the small riches stayed in the family. Imagining Lettie as the thief would be a sorrow similar to those already measured and accepted. Wasn't Dorothea more deserving of an heirloom, more entitled, in fact, than Lettie? Besides, the locket was to serve as an advance, that was all.

Because she was going to make a great deal of money modeling in Chicago, and would bring Mother north, to restaurants with pink tablecloths. (Luc followed her off the train and occupied many of her evenings but understood that she belonged to no one.) As friends appeared in the restaurant to kiss Dorothea's cheek, she would introduce her mother, would move the bud vase aside to smile at her while saying, This is my mother Georgia, visiting from Indiana. Lord, Georgia would say after Lorraine (Dorothea would meet her at their first modeling job, and they would be inseparable) dropped by the table, Lord, what an odd shade of red that child's hair is, Dorothea! And anyone that skinny can't be healthy. I'm Dot now, Mom, Dorothea would laugh, and *honestly*, don't you recognize henna? It's the rage up here, would you care to try it?

Then I said honestly . . . Luc insisted that she replay everything that happened without him, so thoroughly did he long to know her.

Dorothea envisioned herself with elbow-length, spangled gloves while dining, which required editing out because they were a throwback to the forties movies her mother watched with removed passion. Georgia would order the mocha cheesecake, but Dot was vigilant about her figure, though she might steal a bite. Why not, since she would be paying for it?

The unpleasantness, the shriek from downstairs, would last only a minute, then Dorothea could be on the train, and soon thereafter on a runway. She would have spotted the designer in the audience and would have practiced the bored pout the other models had taught her. Vibrant blues, chartreuse silks, styles with cutouts that exposed her belly—she could drape herself with anything, her willowy frame the only redeemable virtue to being a farm girl. Of course the reviewers would describe her red hair as a "flame." A flame, perceiving as they did across the years the burning that drove her, as a child, to unearth the make-up of women in Mother's bridge group when she was taken along to the various houses. She would smear whatever she could find over her face, neck, hands, and chest, the shimmery yellow that made her eyelids into suns, the cold balms sinking into her collarbone, the purple shadows drawn into diamonds on her bare arms. Though aware she would be punished every time, she did not care, simply could not stop herself. It was worth having Mother race in and slap her hand so hard it hurt, just for that instant of shining in a stranger's mirror and finding herself plastered brightly with colors. Huge lips coated red as petals. Eyes made larger with black. She was too drab, far too blank. What a sad day, when Mother could finally afford a babysitter and left her at home. Dorothea raided every sitter's purse, found the hidden jars and tubes of color, and painted herself: joy.

She would install lights around her mirror in Chicago, and might trace in grease pencil the shadows thrown onto her vanity by the pots of shades and removing creams. Creating a history of light, as cast by what transformed her looks. Luc would think she was mad, the good kind of madness, the artist's kind. Certainly Mother should have understood Dorothea's pleasure in women's cosmetic baskets, in finding the makings of a face corralled in the privacy of a bathroom, since Mother had her own cere-monies for seeking comfort: She often opened the larder to stare at its contents, drawing reassurance from the cans of wax beans and packages of oyster crackers that might help them survive the unexpected storm, food a ballast against the unknown. Against abandonment. Quiet gifts, the sense a cupboard or medicine chest gives of *home, everything here.*

Was the coral skirt the best choice? She had selected it after tremendous thought, leaving behind a dozen outfits for Lettie's girls. Her arrival in Chicago had to be light, unburdened.

Mother had made a gentle home, not just a place but a bright enclosure, with things given away if they could enliven a child or a loved one—even Lettie. Mother was childish like that. Dorothea wanted to be a grown-up, which meant, as far as she could divine, blowing asunder whatever blocked one's way—from what? From what and whom one wanted.

Because the *what* and the *whom* were never what you already had, unless you were Mother.

Luc will have commented on the fineness of her skirt's color before their second drink. Their conversation would veer into deeply adult areas, rules of being, with Dorothea offering such jewels as *disillusionment can kill*. Her Daddy had died young of it, after he and Mother lost their jobs at the auto-parts plant for over a year.

Dorothea had walked the pavement with them. The plant in the background was a neutral block with ashes pouring through a chimney. Mother told her to knight Daddy on the shoulder with her picket sign, but his anger put a stop to this fantasy. I'm sorry, James, Georgia said, but she's so small, and her legs hurt, and I don't think it's inviting anyone's generosity to have her out here with the dirty work.

A man called some of the female scabs "rotten split-tails," and Mother loudly asked what he meant. Daddy, red-faced, told her to shut up. Dorothea didn't know what the man meant either, but unlike Mother she had the good sense to keep certain things to herself. One year later, while jumping rope, the answer hit Dorothea. Oh! she said, not missing a beat as she propelled the rope around herself. I know, I know, out of nowhere, oh, went the rhythm of the rope as it slapped into the sky, carving out a capsule of air around her.

The past was not so much a sequence as it was revelations out of sequence that begged to be reordered with a more comfortable balance. In the new, juggled story, Dorothea's jumping rope came before the strike, and she could take her mother aside and whisper to her the secret of how men saw female anatomy, theirs.

The longer the waiting got during the strike, the standing without news or hope, the more hounded Mother looked, open to attack. One scab, standing opposite them on company property, held out a cup of coffee and said, Lady, it's cold and you could use this. I'm only here to feed my kids; they're no older than that little girl you've got there. Can't we be human for a moment?

When Mother went toward him, Daddy leaped forward to smack the coffee through the air. I've got no friends on the other side, and neither does my wife! When a person crosses certain lines, he can't be saved, so shove your coffee up your ass! he shouted.

A person like you, Georgia, you invite sabotage. He was playing you for a fool. For God's sake, know what you want, he fumed the entire night.

Mother poured maple syrup, tapped the summer before from a tree, onto the snow to make candy, rich and shapeless. That was their dinner. I know who I am, James, she said, her hands chapped and scaly from almost freezing. I believe in the gifts of God, and that's why I can feed us out of a tree. What I *want* wouldn't help us right now.

Clasping the *who* and not the *what* to herself kept Mother small, though; it was the sort of sentiment that permitted Lettie to come in and raid the house. Dorothea wished there were arms on the divan so she could slouch over. She had neglected to check the locket for what might be inside. Could she have delivered over her dead father to nestle against the bosom of a stranger? What was taking Mother so long? Was this moment ever going to die and let her get on with the rest of her life? She welcomed the cry: It would hurt for a second, like an inoculation, but the worst part was this anticipating, this praying for the momentary stab of the needle. Find it, find it, she prayed, meaning: Find it gone, already, I'll comfort you, I'll say, You know Lettie, sorry.

Mother intended Dorothea to have the locket; that's why she was downstairs searching.

Dorothea had (had had) the locket.

It was only a matter of rearranging parcels of time, so that intent and result could live in a more peaceful order.

Then this waiting could be cauterized, removed from the chain of events.

The locket was an object *already meant* for Dorothea, for her to convert into her own arrangements for a life.

She wanted a respectable list of accomplishments: to have appeared on three magazine covers; to have worked with Brassman & Fable, the city's top fashion house; to have pivoted on the Fairview runway, the most famous one in town. That would be climbing the heights! One problem would be that she had to regale Luc with things she *had done*, not *would do*. (Wait X amount of time, love, she would tell him on the train, then I *will have...*) Luc would insist that indolence and waiting, facing so many choices, were creating a modern mass suicide, people slaughtered by freedom.

You're absolutely right, she'd say.

Once this waiting on the divan ended, once her mother's cry was over ... yes indeed, Dorothea wouldn't wait a second longer. Life would be a starburst, a radiance flaring and changing.

She already knew that sometimes stories broke apart, as if the lines surrounding events burst from the heat or pressure. There had been that time Dorothea found her mother, who never cried, scaling a trout and sobbing. No fight, no tension preceded it, nothing as far as Dorothea could decipher that might have triggered pain like this. Georgia had scaled many fish before and was not sentimental about preparing animal flesh to eat. Dorothea asked her mother what was wrong.

Look at the poor thing, with those wide eyes! wept Georgia. My God, my God!

Scales flew out from under the knife; Georgia was not pausing in the work that needed doing. The sunlight caught the scales for a flash with the pinks and blues of the outside light, before they were condemned to the mushy pile in the sink. Dorothea put her hand on her mother's arm, but Georgia was too far away to feel her daughter's wish to console.

Dorothea sensed even then that the trout had nothing to do with anything, was only the object that could be pointed to. The crying was about something mysterious, a quiver, maybe stemming from love or a remembered time, or a disappointment that put to the test whether one had the strength to go on or not. Now the mystery was choosing to visit, unsummoned. It could happen to anyone of any age. Never far from mind was that Christmas Eve when Dorothea planned to make blueberry waffles the following day, a surprise, plotted out down to buying the blueberries the day before and hiding them in the freezer. But as she slept, a spider bit her hand before dawn. Mother spent Christmas morning with her in the emergency room of the hospital, feeding her day-old butter cookies with pink and green sugar from the nurses' station as they waited to be seen. One of the nurses, whose nametag said *Anne MacLeod*, had a DVD player that was filling the room with a bagpipe version of "Amazing Grace."

Dorothea had never heard bagpipes before. How triumphant, the music ascending, that unearthly groaning! That blessed nurse, to have a name that sounded so buoyant, so like the heavens! MacLeod, spelled one way, but having a *cloud* within it: It was the first time the sheer loveliness of a name had Dorothea close to tears.

Then Mother opened her mouth and sang her notes without quavering as the bagpipes squeezed, and Mrs. MacLeod lit up as if she had found kin and sister. Dorothea had to glance away. She was beginning to cry from the unnameable beauty of her mother's voice, a shock, how steady it was. Who could have guessed that Georgia would know the lyrics, in their full meaning, had been carrying them around so patiently and could offer them in this frightening moment?

There sat Dorothea, bathed in grace while waiting to find out the fate set for her by the spider of the night.

She closed her eyes, waited.

My Family, Posing for Rodin

Someone ripped my father's apple-tree espalier off his back fence right before Halloween. My brother, Matt, called to tell me. I drove down to Alameda from Sacramento to help him talk our father out of lying in the dark in his room. And I wanted to see the damage for myself. From my second-story window as a child, I had watched the apple branch on one end of the fence grow toward the branch of the thin tree on the opposite side, like the finger of God probing with the slowness of God for the finger of man.

Matt was waiting for me in front of the house, perched on one of the white stone lions. He has the size and manner of a friendly blond crane, and as I stepped from my car, he bounded over and gave me a hug that lifted me off my feet.

"Lara!" he said. "He's been lying in a heap for two days."

"This is probably about Mom, you know," I said. "Finally."

Our father had scarcely mourned her. She died two years ago, in a light-plane crash with her flight instructor from the Alameda Air Station. It might be dawning on my father that his exacting, alluring wife had started an affair with this man after signing up for flying lessons, something that Matt and I sensed from the beginning. We figured it had gone on for a year.

Matt flung his arm around me. "The monsters giving you trouble?"

"No, they're angels. Perfect ones."

I teach ninth-grade science at Lowell Junior High, near the State Capitol. It is true that I am a wonderful teacher on the outside, I cheer them on, I elevate, I entertain, especially on the celebrated day when I show them how to explode gummy-bears in a test tube, but inside I am nowhere near anything of wonder. Inside I am heavy and enlaced with twelve years in a classroom, and my husband, Kevin, is so tired of my complaints that I have a large glass of vodka once the schoolbooks have fallen from my arms in our foyer. I bathe this or that outrage with a clear drink in order to keep my day to myself. From my school window, I see people swollen with furious opinions, trundling across the lawn of the Capitol to listen at the free-speech corner, and as I stand in my room, reciting an amusing anecdote, I am as overstuffed as those wanderers, though the children hardly know it.

A truckload of teenagers screeched past Matt and me, toward Lincoln Park; already the roaming-at-large storm patterns of Halloween were in the cooling air. One boy threatened to throw a pumpkin at us and offered an indecipherable war cry, which Matt returned, smiling. I wanted to hurry inside to Dad.

Matt said he would wait in the back yard so that when I was ready to see the fence, I wouldn't have to face it alone. I climbed the stairs to Dad's room and tapped at his door.

There was no reply.

"Open up," I said.

A muffled sound of refusal.

"Dad! I've come all the way from Sacramento to see you."

He opened the door to the unlit room. He looked like a castaway, unshaven and with an old white shirt rolled above the elbows.

I took his face in my hands as he began to look away. His beard was sprouting fast, white stubble. "Dad," I said. "This isn't like you."

We sat together on the davenport, under the Matisse print of blue people dancing fast. How did I know this wasn't like him? What did I know, anyway? I'd meant that he belonged outside, where he could perform grafts and call plants by their Latin names. The world, I think, is divided between indoor and outdoor people. Everything in the room had been set in place by my mother—the coffee-table book on roses, the Lalique etching of cats on a milk-white vase, the William Morris wallpaper full of dark grapevines—all of it not so much chosen out of fondness as selected for effect.

"I'm fine, darling."

"Matt says you've been in here for two days. Aren't you going to put on your Dracula costume and hand out candy this year?"

"Nah."

"Daddy. Is this about Mother?"

"May she rest in peace. I know I'm in peace without her."

"So this is about her?"

"No. It's about me."

A framed picture of her stayed on his dresser. She shows her teeth in anger and compliance, as if the photographer has said, hey, now, a nice-looking girl like you should be smiling. She is in her silver flight outfit, and her auburn hair brushes her shoulders.

"All right, Dad. This is about you. What's bothering you?"

"You've seen the fence?"

"I wanted to see you first. Have you called the police?"

He laughed. "To say what? You guys are chasing drug dealers, thieves, and murderers, but I've got a dead plant to report?"

"It's called vandalism. Destroying property."

"It's called forget it, because it took thirty years to grow and I can fill out reports until kingdom come and that's not going to replace it."

"I'm going to get two bougainvillea plants," I said, "Tonight. You'll come out and help me plant them?"

"Christ, Lara, what am I, ten years old? I hate reverse psychology. I taught school for forty years, remember? I'll come out when I'm ready. I can't get depressed in my own house?"

"Sure you can, Daddy," I said. I took up his hand and squeezed it. "It's just that I've never seen it from you before."

He nodded and squeezed my hand back. "How about in the morning we run over to the Harvest Nursery? We won't call it starting over or anything stupid. We'll call it 'bougainvillea grows damn fast and will cover the sins of the fence in no time.'"

"I'm going tonight."

"You hate being out on Halloween. And the nursery's closed."

"Payless is open. I can get bougainvillea from the garden center."

"It's getting dark out."

"With a full moon," I said, and kissed him, and I got up to go out and meet Matt by the fence.

Matt was kneeling at the stump of one of the apple trees. The fence looked like a wound without its bandage, wormy and gray, a type of wood I could not identify because I lacked any memory of seeing it bare. A few dying tendrils clung like hooks to the gaps. When I sank next to him, I registered that someone had sawed the apple trees at their roots to make sure they died. A chill started on my skin and vibrated inward. Ants trickled over the mound of earth and white bare bone, as if it were the skull of a freshly dehorned deer.

"Jesus," I said. "Who would do such a thing?"

"People are psycho," said Matt, "and now we get to look at that."

He nodded through the fence at the Millers' yard. A broken tricycle was rusted in place like a tiny mastodon stuck in tar. An old tire—I remembered it from my window as a teenager—was branding a permanent dead ring into the grass.

"Didn't you hear anyone, Matty?" I said. "Someone had a lot to haul away."

"I never saw or heard a thing," he said. "Not a sorry-ass thing."

Matt was twenty-two but still lived at home. I am fifteen years older, and my parents used to introduce him as "our surprise." He had already decided that he would be a multi-millionaire from his web-designing business before age twenty-five, and my father let him roost in the house to save money. Often they worked together in the garden, with that silent work rhythm that alights when a body senses affection from another body in the vicinity.

We sat there waiting for the roots to perform a time-lapse miracle. The deep, narrow lot of my parents showed how my father had preserved each American decade: from the forties, when they bought the house, we still had the parterre vegetable bed. The fifties brought in a walnut tree and rock paths. The sixties to the eighties encompassed life as a tropical-dream: gardenias, azaleas. My mother's attempt to add her mark had been a redwood burl table from a tourist's shack along the Pacific Coast Highway, but it vanished, and so did her wooden sign reading, "The DiBiasi Family," which Matt burned, calling it "too hobbity." In the nineties and onward into the time of Mother's affair with the flight instructor and crash, our father was unthinkingly attracted to buoyancy with spikes: birds-of-paradise, lilies-of-the-Nile.

"You going to wear the usual tonight?" I asked him.

He grinned. "Sure." I once screamed that his music was splitting my brain, and he bought me a rubber head mask with an axe in the middle, which he reclaimed and wore every year. I would be sad when he stopped.

"I'm going out to buy a bougainvillea at Payless, and Dad won't be able to stand the thought of me trying to plant it by myself," I said.

"A good idea," said Matt. "A useful, constructive Halloween. I hope to drink enough to pass out but not stay sick in the morning."

"That's a fine plan," I said.

A pack of his friends arrived and signaled to him from the side gate. All of them struck me as mysterious—pale junk-food eaters who earned enormous checks for what they did with computers. They were good about carrying home any incapacitated comrades and dumping them on front porches.

"I'll be home at a decent hour to see if Dad's emerged," he said. "I need a break from putting food in the hallway to lure him out."

"I'll give it a shot," I said. "Don't get killed."

That first drop of ink that announces the night was spreading over the sky as I aimed down Pearl Street toward the South Shore Center. I could get to Payless and return before dark. I told myself to relax; so what if night fell while I joined everyone heading to Payless for beer and candy? Although I am an indoor person, like my mother, and though I believe that everyone selects things out of the chaos whether from the inside or outside and arranges them and calls the result a story or a home, outdoor people are less afraid of the night, and I aspire to this.

I was glad to be enclosed in my car but out in the open. My tire caught a smear of pumpkin innards, and I slowed down. Alameda's city streets are shaded with elms, oaks, and fruit trees, and it could well be this that I admire most—"Alameda" means "a tree-lined place." Almost nothing—no one and no geography—offers what it truly is, in plain view. The salted ocean water mixed with the Bay breezes to scour our air free to receive a full charge of sunlight. The gardens here thrived. I loved Alameda for being an island and could not figure out why everyone didn't enjoy it more than Berkeley or Oakland or San Leandro. Perhaps the roads felt like canals that might lock, not enough like open, swift roads. Perhaps people looked on a map and thought Alameda was shaped too much like a pistol, with the Naval and Air stations at the muzzle. The Ballena Bay keys form a trigger. My childhood house is in the handgrip.

The narrowness of the streets caused most of them to be one-way but forever changing, and I often got lost in my hometown. Instead of staying on Otis, I curved up past Powell and found myself navigating the comb-shaped waterway that Alameda tucks inland.

I read this as a sign that I was meant to weave through the residential section near Cedar and Walnut, where it happened that my first true love, Michael Nicolini, lived with the woman he had left me for. I liked that I still loved him, with my desires filed down into a shard that I could keep embedded in my heart to prod me without harming my marriage to Kevin. Whenever I had a fight with Kevin or needed some vaporous comfort, I would think of Michael.

What harm there? Most people carry some torch or other, which time and clear-sightedness reduce to a very low burning. Fantasies form an inner ballast—don't they? Yesterday, after pouring my vodka, I went to curl up in the bedroom, and the heaviness of the quilt folded at the foot of the bed revealed a cache of porno magazines. I'd never seen them before. Kevin must have forgotten to hide them elsewhere. They weren't *Playboy* or *Penthouse* but more hardcore stuff, which aroused me before I shoved the magazines back under the quilt, feeling odd. I wandered into the kitchen and kept my coat on to look as if

I'd just walked in, and I was still at the table when Kevin came home. The magazines disappeared by bedtime. We talked about his efforts to make law partner and fell asleep without touching. I dreamed of a man pounding inside a woman, his mouth clutching her neck.

I only saw my ex, Michael, by chance when I visited Alameda, and when I did, it was usually at a distance. He would wave warmly, and so would his wife, Angela. Their house was on Willow, and I used the lowering cover of night to park there and look. Brick Americana, with a galloping-horse weathervane. The porch light was on to welcome trick-or-treaters. Maybe they had a child now? My heart thumped. If he and Angela had begun a family, my haphazard dreams about Michael were in danger of being torn from me as delusional. Yellow light emanated around the jagged teeth of the jack-o'-lantern in their window.

Michael was calm of nerves and knew what he wanted and generally, serenely, acquired it. The furniture would be spare and clean of line, an only slightly more solid version of air and light. Chairs of a single wave-curve. Glass lamps with the brass innards showing.

Nothing like the fussy house I'd grown up in; Matt and Dad and I were these squiggly living things put there to sharpen my mother's belief that people existed merely to encroach on taste and beauty. I was bringing weight rather than lightness to my own home, full of dust-catcher gifts and brocade sofas, expensive curtains and display cases, and cruets, tureens, and butter plates, kitchen clutter that Kevin and I never used.

Around Angela's throat would be a necklace of light blue stars, from his Milanese grandmother. It had once been around my neck.

I looked away from the house, through my windshield, up at the night. Someone had swabbed glycerin over the moon. It looked back at me, blank but bright.

I thought I saw a car with Matt and his friends, and I knocked hard on the window and waved. But it wasn't Matt; the car was driven by a skeleton, with a werewolf in the backseat with Munch's Scream. They hooted and grabbed at themselves and waved wildly back.

A troupe of angels, ballerinas, and gypsies passed by on the sidewalk, with a grown-up leading them house to house. They swung plastic pumpkins and carried brown sacks decorated with crayon. No one was pushing or shoving. Pleasant family life—costumes thought up and finished on time, the holiday met. This was the day you could knock on strangers' doors, and they would say how scary you looked and reward you for that, and you could revel in being scared right along with them, which neutralized everyone's fear. What was it that I hated about Halloween? It could be a sweet, brave way to address a year's worth of nights.

Cars like metal tanks hurled past, loud music on the radios. Though I told myself to be careful pulling away, I almost knocked into a car surging from behind. Shaking, I eased back into traffic.

But my mind stayed back at Michael's house, wondering if he and Angela had had a child, and when I looked forward I inhaled sharply and slammed on my brake. I hadn't noticed the stoplight and kept skidding forward until I tapped the fender of the car in front, forcing me into the kind of coincidence that the world happily delivers up over and over: The car was the one with the skeleton, the werewolf, and the Scream. They wheeled around in their seats at me. I gave a shrug to show that I was sorry and was left with no idea where to focus.

The Scream leapt out and came around to stare where our bumpers touched. He leaned over and clapped his hands to the sides of his head, an imitation of the painting, and staggered. He tapped on my windshield until I looked at him, and he shook a finger at me and waited until I smiled feebly. I didn't know what else to do, other than try to will the light into changing. The Scream leaned over to stare into my face, and when he caught my eye, he planted a kiss on my windshield, only the thickness of glass away, before running back into his friend's car in time for the green signal.

They howled with laughter, and the skeleton pumped his fist at me and immediately a horn blew from the line-up of cars behind; I talked myself into lifting my foot off the brake. As I passed below the streetlight, I could see the wet smudge left on my windshield.

I circled away from the South Shore Center to lose them. I would go to Payless, buy my bougainvillea, return home, rescue my father, and start the fence on the journey back to being a work of art. A slick of sweat was on the wheel, and I punched the radio dial four times before I found the classical station—a Handel harp concerto.

The music was floating but rich, choir-like, and seemed written by angels, for them, about them. Sound, idea, and audience in harmony. I had a stab of envy for people like Michael, who lived in Alameda because he adored it here, who had a house that *was* him, who was with the person

109

he could not fathom being without. I once asked him if he ever thought of me, and out of politeness, he said that he recalled me fondly. What else could he have said? He was with the person he loved, and their days grew out of that: His insides were the same as his outsides.

It was my mother who led me to recognizing this. One afternoon, she and I went to the Palace of the Legion of Honor in San Francisco to see Rodin's statue, The Kiss, and my mother stared at it until the guards wondered if she would do something crazy. The tears made straight silver tracks down her cheeks. I asked why she was crying, and she said I wouldn't understand. She wasn't sure she could explain the reason so well herself.

I couldn't fathom her tears until much later, when I realized the truth about Michael: If Rodin were to do an artwork of Angela and him, it would look like The Kiss. Everything about them—desires, dreams—created what they did, the whole outside of them, both the sum and the minute workings of their lives. The man and woman in Rodin's Kiss were purely the wanting of each other: When everything about your outer form cannot be distinguished from your insides, you are a register of all that is humanly divine.

The harp concerto drifted to its quavering end. Merging into the lane headed for the left turn into the shopping center caught me in the midst of the crowd stopping for booze, inch-long chocolate bars, and last-minute outfits for their crying kids. In the parking lot, ghosts and gypsies ran around, ignoring their parents calling at them to come back, and some teenagers done up like Kiss were smoking pot and leaning against an old

Saturn. A couple not in costume was necking inside their car, and a seizure of longing obliged me to glance away.

The garden area of Payless was outside the sliding front doors. Stacks of tile plaques sold fast here, with homey sayings about growth, flowers, God—things my father believed in but would rather be dead than put in his landscape. He despised the unearthy cuteness of ceramic rabbits and frogs. He liked naked angels if they appeared to have weathered a few storms.

The lights inside the store exposed everything, and I could look through the windows and see the milling people, many of them wrapped in sheets, buying wine and cartons of cigarettes. Long lines formed at the cash registers. Some clerks were in the spirit of the night, wearing fright masks and witch's pointed hats. Whenever the pneumatic doors slid open, sneezing and coughing billowed out. Matt's Theory of the One-Hundredth Cougher holds that a crowd anywhere, whether in a church, movie theater, bank, or store, is required to answer a single cough with one hundred.

A bank of pink-and-orange bougainvilleas stood in small black tubs against the garden-center wall. It's a plant worth admiring—the heart-shaped flowers are delicate but tough; they will drape their color over any fence or wall and outlast seasons. Bougainvillea grows so fast that you can almost watch it embalm whatever you want covered. It is a hot-climate vegetable paint, but thinking of it as a quick, cheap cover made my enthusiasm flag. What was that, compared to an espalier whose virtue was that it had been years in the making?

How intricate the espalier had been, year by year: a breathing Japanese screen. At other times, I imagined that

111

it was an unfurled bolt of dotted Swiss that could muffle the sound of my parents arguing; at least they saved their quarrels for behind closed doors and never fought in public. The white apple blossoms with gold stamens came and went, the dwarf green fruit waited for its time to return. Nothing in a given moment ever seemed to move. But then three decades went by and left behind dozens of entwining arms that said: Here's a happy house with an heirloom floral quilt. You could watch everyone intuit the links—beautiful growth, solid history, solid family.

I moved from the sixteen-dollar starter vines to some larger tubs with bougainvilleas the size of young trees, propped tall with stakes. I chose two plants and pulled off a few brown stems; my father taught me that most of gardening was cutting away the dead stuff.

The clerk for the outdoor department leaned with his elbows on the counter, talking to a skinny blonde with a tattoo of barbed wire around her upper arm. She was in a sleeveless T-shirt, though the night was saturated with the first warning of autumn. Kohl marks encircled their eyes, and the boy had slicked enough grease in his hair to have it standing on end.

"Excuse me," I said. "I need help with those bougain-villeas."

He glared at me. I had interrupted his conversation. An empty Payless bag turned end over end in the wind as if it were collecting Halloween air at ground level to haul it back into the sky.

"You in a rush?" he said, narrowing his eyes so that the black lines around them joined.

"No. Just—just ready to leave."

"So leave."

The girl gave a horsy laugh. "Some party to get to, sweetheart?" she said. "You're looking pretty booty."

I was in standard uniform—jeans, white blouse, loafers, leather jacket. "No," I said, and stopped. I had no idea what she meant. Through the glare of the interior of the store, I saw the skeleton, the werewolf, and the Scream, with six-packs under their arms. They were next at their register. If I paid right now and carried my plants to the car, I would be on my way, a step ahead of them. I could also walk out right now, but Matt would scold me and say, "Repeat to yourself: I have a right to be outside after dark."

I stepped toward the bougainvillea and pointed. "These two are just right," I said. "How much?"

"'Just right.' That how you talk?" said the clerk. "Like Martha fucking Stewart?"

When I glanced again into the store, the skeleton was holding out his wallet. Their beer was on the conveyor. Then they saw me. So it was true; it was as easy to see out as in. The skeleton grinned.

I went to the bougainvillea, and my hand shook as I checked the price tags. When I lifted one tub, I almost dropped it. It was heavy. Straggling roots stuck out from the drainage holes, and the thin trunk and showy green bracts lashed gently over me as I carried it to the counter. People were coming in and out of the sliding doors. A smile meant nothing, maybe the palest, palest recognition.

"The price tag says thirty dollars," I said. "I'm going to put the money on the counter, and if you're not going to tell me what the tax is, I'll come back in the morning and settle with the manager."

The girl with the barbed-wire tattoo cracked up. "You a lawyer or something? Or do you keep a two-by-four up your ass for fun?"

"I am going to pay right now, and leave," I said. I set the bougainvillea down—I would return for the other one in the morning, when All Saints' Day arrived clear and light. But the red strap of my shoulder bag slipped, and I knelt down to retrieve my purse, losing time, and I fumbled with the clasp. The clerk and his girlfriend were amused. There were no other customers; who bought plants on Halloween? By the time I placed thirty dollars on the counter, thinking that he could pocket the money and tell the manager I had stolen the bougainvillea, that I should demand a receipt, the doors slid open and out came a mother and daughter, followed by the skeleton, the werewolf, and the Scream, right as I put my hands around the tub, ready to lift it. I was not surprised to discover that they were friends with the clerk and his girlfriend—everyone but my father and me was in league with the festival of the night.

My knees flexed and I stood, and there we all were, out of our cars in front of Payless. The bougainvillea quivered; I couldn't hold it steady. The flowers shook in a blown-up halo around me.

"Yo, fucked up you have to spend Halloween here, bitch." The skeleton spoke to the male clerk but stared in my direction. "Hello, baby," he said to me. "Why the face? Don't you like Halloween?"

I made two terrible mistakes, one right after the other. The first was to answer truthfully. "I don't like Halloween, no," I said before glancing toward the parking lot to gauge how far I had to go to reach the safety of my car. I let them read my fearful heart.

"Nooo," said the skeleton, imitating my quaking voice.

People continued entering and exiting the store. I told myself that these boys in costume were not going to harm me. I turned to leave.

"Yeah, it's taking it too far when you got people stealing," said the clerk.

I looked back at him and said, "I paid you thirty dollars." I pointed at the bills on the counter. "You should give me a receipt."

"Ooo," said the werewolf, "she bites."

The clerk clamped my bills between his teeth.

"She punks you where you work, man, and asks for a receipt," said the skeleton. "Do we have one for the damage to our car?"

"Damage?" said the clerk's girlfriend.

"She's not only a thief, she's a hit-and-run asshole, too. She hit our car!" said the Scream.

"Busy night!" said the clerk. "She looks so collected and ordinary."

"I tapped your bumper. That's what bumpers are for."

"I'd love to tap your bumpers, lady," said the Scream.

Their laughter gusted against my back as I picked up the bougainvillea. I knew that I shouldn't run, but walking as if I were not trying to hurry was more difficult than I imagined.

But then I was away from the light and other people, putting the bougainvillea in the trunk of my car, and that was what they had been waiting for: for me to think that I was safe, simply because I was out of their direct line of vision. Simply because I wanted my safety to be true.

They held me back while the Scream went to work shredding the bougainvillea. My attempt to paint over the fence was going to last minutes, not decades. The heart-shaped flowers rained over the back of my car and onto the asphalt and over me as if I were this person I vaguely knew but whose life I was not actually living. The Scream was yelling that I'd damaged his property, and now he would damage mine.

They had me hidden between two parked cars. The werewolf ripped at my blouse while the other two held my arms, and his teeth sank into the soft flesh right above my breast. Almost as bad as the pain was the feel of his hair and exhaling nose against my skin. My knees buckled, and a carload of teenagers screeched up and came to my rescue, but I never saw their faces. I finished kneeling and must have fainted when I hit the ground.

I needed twenty stitches in the hospital. I awoke to see Matt at my bedside, wearing the mask with the axe to cheer me, and we laughed before tearing up. I had not yet examined the scar over my breast, but I was rehearsing the strange truth for Kevin: Under the full moon, my chest was bared, and someone in disguise gouged me. There are more germs in the human mouth than in the mouth of any other animal.

"Dad's on his way," said Matt. "You didn't have to get so drastic to get him out of his room, Lara. But it worked."

I closed my eyes and gave him a half-smile.

"We called Kevin. He's driving down."

When Kevin arrived, I would say: Throw out the vodka. And I won't spend another day in our house with its nice drapes and gourmet kitchen if we can't touch each other anymore.

The nurse brought me a glass of water and laughed at Matt's axe. She had a weightlifter's body. She told Matt if he had a headache and wanted that thing removed, he'd have to get in line in the emergency.

Matt steadied the straw for me to drink from the glass of water before setting it down. "Here comes Dad," he said.

My father, clean-shaven, in a suit and tie, was hurrying to his injured daughter, her blood continuing to seep through a gauze patch.

I did have a chance later to see "The Scream" by Edvard Munch. It was on display during the Summer Olympics in Atlanta, and there was a starkness to the fear in it, a redness and reverberation, a sense of hopeless vertigo, that is lost in the many replicas now—punching dolls, ties, and holiday cards meant to signify stress and annoyance. None of those knock-offs can match the power of the original: A distant figure wavers as if it is the scream come loose from the screamer. I was alone at the exhibition at the Olympics; though Kevin and I stay in touch and are not yet divorced, we separated several months after my accident. We remark how curious it is that we are better friends now.

My clock-shaped, rust-colored scar seems in no hurry to go away. My breast aches particularly in the cold.

I still do not know how to leave teaching. I am doing some good; I no longer bathe my insides with poisonous vodka; I wish I felt goodness within me.

My father admitted one day that he knew about my mother and the flight instructor. Matt and I thought we were so clever, but we were way off—the affair had gone on a good long while. My father mentioned suspecting about some other men, too, but two years after my mother died, when he decided to sort through her things, nothing had prepared him for the boxes of love letters he discovered—more men and fervor, more secrets than he imagined. Rodin doing my family: Man trying to embrace woman, woman looking away transfixed with love letter, son loping toward computer, son-in-law trying to embrace the family's daughter, daughter faking affection for students, daughter gazing desperately, in her dreams, toward old boyfriend. Old boyfriend gone, absorbed into The Kiss.

But every family also has its synchronous poses:

Not long after my mother and I saw the Rodin show in the Palace of the Legion of Honor, I came down sick. She brought me water in a tumbler while I lay in bed. I remember the ridges of the blue and yellow bands around the cold glass and the lance of orange light trimming the parting between my curtains; I contain everything because my mother bending close to me was my statue, my kiss, a pure moment, with her thinking of nothing but the truth of her loving me right now, water, child, orange light, a cure. If my mother were alive, I would say to her, "You cried at the Rodin statue because the man and woman needed no adornment to show their passion."

I was not surprised to see The Kiss included at the Olympics' art exhibit. It had not changed, of course. It never will: muscles in a close weave with other polished muscles. Hidden tongues entwined. Looking at it, a voyeur in front of a privacy with nothing to hide, I knew that when I returned to my hotel, I would call my father and say, "It was you, wasn't it, Dad? After you found those letters?"

Glimpsing outside our family window, you wondered why everything should look abundant when you had so little. You looked at the espalier, the weight of thirty years made elegant as can be. You're the one who grabbed up a saw, and under the cover of night, you cut that showpiece off at the roots.

- desire turning adults into children

Fig. 4. *I waited for Something One & Only, not realizing it was far off, wondering what was taking me*

He said you are my immortal X1000 & then WHERE DID YOU LIE

A Simple Affair

Maria is getting ready, in front of the bathroom sink. After she and Robert tour a house that's suddenly on the market, he's going to drive her to a restaurant operated by the blind. She has an assignment to write about it. He perches on the edge of the bathtub, watching her "put on her beauty face"—that's the expression her mother from Buenos Aires always used.

She gargles loudly with mouthwash, a childish aria; she's trying to amuse him.

"Stop," he says. *Stop that.* "That's the sound people make when they're about to drown."

She spits out the mouthwash and looks at him. He hasn't been a lifeguard in decades. "Did you ever lose anyone?" They're both on their second marriage, they've been together ten years, and she's never asked him about his summers when he was young, at the edge of the water.

"No," he says. "Yes. Once. A girl in the surf was grinning at me, and I was screaming, *Turn around, get out.* A wave was gathering force and roaring up. It hit her from behind, and she got carried away, and I swam and almost caught her, but her head bashed against a rock. An orange

FIG. 5 (OPPOSITE). *I rode an elephant in exotic lands; I brought home an adamant sense that language lives high overhead, with an animal below.*

mess with strings came out of her mouth, and I don't know if it was a jellyfish, or part of her."

"I'm sorry. But most days were peaceful?"

"Yes. But not really. We'd start wishing for some real action until we realized that meant we were waiting for a near-death thing."

"I'm sorry about that, too."

"We never got disappointed. People wouldn't stop with their flinging around, acting dangerous or stupid. Actual dying didn't happen very often, but almost dying happened all the time."

Maria rents a room plus bath in San Francisco because she writes for the *Chronicle*. A dying profession, a dying news source, but it is what she knows. At night, alone in her bed, on a third floor of a wooden Victorian, she puts herself away like a plate on its high shelf. Robert is here this weekend, but during workdays he stays in their bungalow in Sacramento, where he is a lobbyist on behalf of California's waterways. People imagine that their weekends return them to the frenzy of their first days together. But doesn't passion mean you can't bear to stay away? Maria left the *Sacramento Bee* three years ago for a better job in San Francisco and, she thought, the first strike in getting them closer to the coast, the natural result of Rob's jokes about not being able to breathe inland. It's not an unusual scramble of work and geography, with a man and a woman returning to each other with too many solitary hours, long nighttimes, muffled around themselves.

Several of Rob's fellow lobbyists have opened a firm in San Francisco, and Maria is eager for him to dust off his law degree and join them. Rob said himself once or twice that he might do more for the water by prosecuting offenders, big-gun stuff, rather than scuttling around the Capitol in pursuit of slippery lawmakers.

Maria sweeps up her black hair with a rhinestone butterfly. Robert helps her with the clasp. She must remind him that he should get ready himself, a tie if he wants, although the evening at the restaurant of the blind should be a casual, ordinary affair.

She wears a silk shift, green. Teardrop pearl earrings, low-heeled pink sandals. She grabs her shawl (another castoff from her Argentine mother), the white one with fringe that used to make Robert ask, Was she going to burst into song, or kneel and pray? After viewing a house for sale at her insistence, they'll head north into Benicia to pick up their friends, Nell and Jim, and then circle all the way back. Nell is recovering from lung cancer, Jim's car is in the shop, and an adventure in a dark restaurant might soak up her dark moods; this will need to be one of those elastic days that stretches the hours as far as they will go.

Maria is almost pressed against the mirror to see well enough to etch black lines around her eyes. A year has passed since her surgery to correct a turning-in of the left one, a return to the weak muscles and double vision of her childhood. *People wore gray registers of themselves when I was young. Objects swam in their own reflections. I can't believe that's back to haunt me, Rob.*

"Let's get this over with," says Robert.

It's a Sunday, but any hour is of a Sunday to the lost souls wandering across Haight Street, thirty years too late for the party. *You know why they don't get bored milling back and forth, Maria? Same reason a fish can swim in a tank without getting crazed. Their memory banks are good for two minutes, and so they get to one end and turn around and everything's new to them.* They do entertain each other.

The house Maria stumbled upon is in the Mission district—the mortgage will be a stretch, but it's within reach, sort of—the first genuine gift to appear. The owner is pregnant and eager for a sale, but when Maria said, *She liked me, she's holding out a day longer for our response,* Robert's reply was, *Like, schmike, it'll go to the highest bidder.* Her face burned. *No, if we match the top bid, it'll go to us, because that woman was fond of me.*

"Perfect," says Robert, as they turn onto 22nd Street to park. "If we get the house, we don't have to go far to post bail bonds."

She gets out and slams the door. The exterior of the house is shabby. But inside, as they climb the white-carpeted stairs into a high-ceilinged living room emblazoned a bold red, with window seats at the curved glass, she can read Robert's silence as being identical to what had first enveloped her: He's instantly in love. The kitchen is mint-green. The Victorian moldings have been kept. No drabness was allowed to settle.

When the owner, Rosalie, hurries over and says, *Oh, finally, good, he's with you,* Maria introduces Robert, who shakes Rosalie's hand and comments with polite enthusiasm about the house. But then he wanders off. He's usually the friendly one; it's no accident that he's a lobbyist. Maria's the shy one. But she won over Rosalie by admiring her ceramics, especially the French Quimper set, and they laughed at the cavorting animals on the Mexican tureen.

Maria has, again, a sharply etched vision of inhabiting this home with Robert; she can see them moving about the rooms. She's calling out from the pantry: *Robert? Is that you? Did you remember to buy olives?* A bouillabaisse is on the stove. Her own ceramics are in the display case.

But Robert is signaling that he wants to leave. Maria lingers on the back porch with Rosalie, where they discuss the immense messy work that went into the tiny lily pond. When she glares over her shoulder, Rob is near the front door. In his suit, he seems ready to take her to a dance. They're elaborately overdressed. They do look lovely together.

At a nearby café, he says pointedly, "I can afford to buy lunch." But then he's his old self. He converses with the boy taking the order. He laments that they will not be able to buy a nice meal whenever they desire at this genuine neighborhood place. By the time the turkey sandwiches arrive, he's discovered that the cook is going through a divorce. Rob decides that today is evidence that bargains are still to be found in this city, and he's so cheered that he calls for a beer for himself and a white wine for Maria.

"I don't want any wine, Robert. Christ. It's two in the afternoon."

But he buys a glass and sets it down. Floating on the disc of the wine's surface is a reduction, marble-sized, of the hot fluorescence overhead. She didn't order it, and she's not going to drink it. Rosalie will be speaking into the answering machine in her room—it could be happening right this second—that ten bids are being considered; where is Maria's? *I can't swing it alone, Rosalie; we're going to miss out, I'm afraid.*

"Maria. It means that decent places are out there, when we're really ready to go ahead," he says.

"No," says Maria. "No." She has a plain sensation of a turning point, something passing, a hesitation that will fortify the wrong types of surrender. The wine shimmers untouched, and she says, "There's this old joke. A guy is drowning in a river, and a man with a boat says, 'Get in,' but the guy says no, God will save him. A pilot in a helicopter drops a rope, but the guy yells he can't grab it; he's waiting for God. He drowns. When he gets to heaven, he says, 'God? Why didn't You save me?' And God says, 'I sent you a boat and a helicopter, what more do you want?'"

They climb into the car to crawl along with the flat, slow traffic of Valencia Street. "Whatever the hell that means," Robert says. He asks if she'd mind if he skipped dinner at the restaurant for the blind, which, sorry, he fears is another sign of the city getting too trendy for words. The workweek is going to be crushing; he should head back to Sacramento while it's early. He'll drop her at her place. She needs to get over her reluctance to drive on her own; her surgery is long since over. Nell and Jim will keep her company, and frankly she has more patience for Nell than he does.

He grabs her hand and holds onto it as he escorts her to her car, the smallest and simplest of touches, but a shock blazes through her at how starved they've been—it's been ages. His raven hair has gone white in places, and his skin is sun-weathered. She's quit fighting for him to exchange his wire-rimmed spectacles for a new model; he protests he's comfortable with what he has. *They make you look old, and don't tell me that forty-nine is old, Rob.* He looks near

128

tears. "Being mindful that at my age I can't just say bang, I'll start over—well, it doesn't mean I don't love you."

"I know. You're very sweet, really."

"I'm killing you with that," he says, kissing her forehead. "Goodbye, Maria."

Alone on the 80 Freeway, she veers away from two cars that drift out of their lanes, the average number of near sideswipes, close calls. The signs fly by: *Dried Fruits. Squash. Fresh Blood—Great Sausage!*

It's only recently that her *waiting* has run up against his *stopping*. Every time she's offered to quit her job and move back to Sacramento, he reminds her that San Francisco has given her great stories, and she's poised to make the transition to blogs or whatever. She's won prizes. A magazine award—a Maggie, which called to mind Maggie Smith, for some reason, and *The Lonely Passion of Judith Hearne*—for a piece she wrote on some earthquake survivors in the Marina, which now strikes her as predatory and cheap, like claiming to be close to someone who's died in order to be sanctified by anguish in the eyes of others. *What did it feel like, to lose everything? May my photographer take a shot of you with nothing but the clothes on your back?* The thrill of a disaster's proximity, the arousal brought on by the calamity she's safe from. At the awards banquet, her colleagues had teased her about being offered a year abroad in the news bureau in Madrid.

"Goddamn it," Beth had hissed. "You Spanish types get all the perks."

"She's Spanish?" Greg, the business editor, had practically shouted. "What kind of Spanish name is O'Hara?"

"Her skin is paler than mine," Beth had said, "and she has blue eyes, for crying out loud."

"You know what they call Argentines?" Maria had offered, embarrassed. "Germans who act like Italians but speak Spanish. I'm all mixed up."

But Rob, I don't want to go to Madrid. Why do you keep pushing for that? I'm sick of my whole Spanish pose. I'm American. My father is Irish. If I get assigned one more folk festival because I can lumber half-assed through the language, I'll choke. Do you not want me in Sacramento because you're having an affair?

That's a good one. I can't imagine anyone better than you. That means I don't want to be responsible for ruining your promise. I don't want to be a lawyer, Maria. My job has become staying out of your way.

She's praying that Nell will behave. Other journalists will be at the restaurant for the blind, including Benedikt Dvořák, a Czech ophthalmologist with a practice in Boston who has gone on to be famous, in the manner of Oliver Sacks or A.R. Luria. His article "Me Alone at Night," about a woman with night blindness, has been reprinted in anthologies. There'll be writers and bloggers and Internet geniuses from *The International Herald Tribune*, *The Washington Post*, and possibly *Time*.

In the worst stages of Nell's chemotherapy, she'd shriek at Maria, or Robert, or her husband, Jim. She threw food at the walls, called Maria a hooker, told Jim he was getting balder than she was. Then she'd weep. One morning, she took Jim's rifle and blew out a window. Jim begged Maria not to abandon them. So far, she's willing to consider that Nell's behavior is a forgivable, animal shriek. They spent lots of time together in San Francisco before Nell and Jim escaped north, to more reasonable prices, but Maria wonders, as she passes the Richmond refinery with its butter-colored storage tanks, if this new distance might not have allowed them to end their friendship quietly, before Nell rips it to shreds. Many intimacies are allowed a peaceable finish—are preserved, really—by the forces of geography.

Maria rolls down her window to let in Benicia's coolness from the wet ribbon of the Carquinez Strait. She likes coasting down Main Street with its antique shops, near the old State Capitol building. Benicia is an artists' town, except that tucked away halfway between San Francisco and Sacramento it seems in the process of a long exhalation, a sitting back from itself; everyone must drive elsewhere to work. Jim is a loan officer at Wells Fargo Bank in San Francisco, and Nell, before her illness, oversaw photo e-filing at the *Chronicle*. There's a brave prettiness, doors with stained glass, ice-cream parlor chairs studded with needles from the evergreens, but it doesn't mean the residents aren't wary that a change of winds might bring vapors from the refinery.

When she pulls alongside Jim's sloping lawn, he's outside, waiting.

"Hell," he says, the moment she steps from her car. She drapes her arm around his shoulder—he isn't much taller than she is—and his head with its stiff, straw-colored hair, as if it's broken on its stem, lolls against her neck. He encircles and clutches her waist.

"How bad is it?" she says. She's startled to be close enough to see what appears to be a thumbprint where his soft spot was; who pressed him there so that it never healed?

"All I did, I swear, Maria, was remind her you'd be here any second and it was time to get ready, but we seem stuck always inside a nightmare, and she poured another merlot and started ranting about you—"

"How many has she already drunk?"

He drops his arm and steps away as if he needs an immediate longer view of her. "It's not as if you're a teetotaler, Maria."

"We all remember the evening I threw up in your bathroom, Jim."

"What are a few trade secrets among friends?"

"Right. Shall we go inside?"

"If you'd arrived five minutes earlier, you'd've walked in right as she grabbed a knife off the counter and threw it, maybe she was meaning to throw it at the wall, not at my head, but it didn't stick. It fell behind the couch and she started roaring totally amused and I said, 'you fucking mad woman' and came out here and Maria of the magnificent timing, the cavalry, drove up."

"You said she was ranting about me. What did I do or not do, Jim?"

"Join the club. This isn't about you. Cancer makes her mad. Being too sick to leave home makes her mad. I make her mad just by breathing, I guess."

"Then let's tell her I'm here to get her out of the house."

The knife is lying like a dead silver fish behind the living room's couch, and Nell is enthroned in the rocking chair, smiling toward this little murder mystery theater scene. On the picture window behind the couch, the sun has leaned its boiling head. One leg is tucked underneath her and with her other leg she's rocking hard enough so that her bare foot thumps on the carpet. Maria pulls her shawl around herself and says, "Why don't we find a nice dress for you to wear, Nell?"

"Oh, Miss Es-pan-eesh girl blondie who looks like a model, she doesn't like how I'm dressed."

"Nell! Keep it up, let's get rid of all our friends one by one. Maria looks nice because she wants to take you out," says Jim.

Nell cackles and says, "Maria looks nice because she always looks nice, ee-spicey nicey. Here's a story. We're summoned for a dinner party by this girl whose mother is from South America and grew up in a cardboard box but put on lipstick and winked and before you can say 'Eva Peron,' she marries an Irish fireman in San Francisco, this girl decides Mom is exotic, I mean who gets raised in cardboard. The girl's got her American lunchbox and fruit loops and Barbie, but hey, let's cash in on the mom, so the half-Spanish girl writes stories that sell for gen-you-wine money about ee-span-eesh people like she's one of them instead of like the rest of us."

"Shut up, why don't you," says Maria.

"But you're missing the best part! There's this dinner party, see, a command performance, with the girl and her husband cooking for three days, and it's of course South American, muy muy ow-ten-tee-coo, and this is way before I got sick, but I suggest at this party that suicide is a reasonable choice for a person to make, and the hostess my friend declares, *It never is.*"

"I still believe that, Nell," says Maria. She and Robert had shaped fruits out of marzipan, grilled fish that had bathed for two days in zinfandel, bought a pastry torch to caramelize the skin over the pudding, studied Argentine cookbooks, and all anyone wanted to do was battle about suicide. Several of the guests still are not speaking. She and Robert had held hands under the table. "There'll be lots of reporters at the restaurant. It'll be a goddamn fun time. Get dressed, Nell."

Nell adjusts the scarf covering her scalp, screws her eyes shut, and apes a blind person using a fork. Her teeth have a faint violet stain. Nell once mentioned wanting to be cremated rather than having a stranger open her on a slab, tabulating her sins, noting that the yellow fat was evidence of steak medallions, ice cream, summer nights that refused to end, wine straight to fat cells, her inability to restrain herself, to tip her discipline "the other way."

"There's a rumor that Dr. Benedikt Dvořák will be there," says Maria. "Maybe you saw him on *60 Minutes*."

Nell's head rears back with a new blast of laughter. "He's got that stupid accent so he can seduce women."

"I think he really is Czech," says Jim. "The real item."

"I get it." Nell points at Jim and shouts, "Czech," and points at Maria and shouts, "Mate!"

"Okay," says Maria, standing. "Live, die, whatever you want, Nell. Goodbye."

"Wait! Don't you want to know the end of the story? Because you don't know, Maria. Trust me."

Her hand is on the doorknob, and Jim is begging his wife to stop.

"We're driving home after the suicide feast with its tons of food, it's like, top this one, gang, five-course reminder that we'll always outdo you, and I ask Mr. Jim to whom I've been married for fifteen years if he ever pretends in the dark that I'm some other woman, and he says, 'No.'"

Jim goes to the rocking chair and leans close to Nell's face and barks, "Stop this." He grasps the collar of her shirt but she pushes him away without breaking the rhythm of her rocking. Maria tells herself to leave before it's too late, but she's frozen to the spot.

"He says, 'No, lambkins, darling, gorgeous, I think only of you-oo-oo,' but I keep on him, 'Everyone pretends now and then, it's normal. Who is it for you when the lights are out?'"

Jim sinks on the couch, folds his hands.

"He says, 'That Maria O'Hara, she's smart, she's a beauty, she'd be dangerous if she knew it, I've always been a little in love with that one.'"

Maria cautions herself against breaking into a run on her way to the car. She hears Jim behind her and turns to him. He's a man emerged from a cave, squinting. "I swear it would be easier if she'd died," he says, staring at the ground. "I spent lots of time picturing myself in my black suit at her funeral. Crying. Kissing her in the coffin. Telling everyone how much I loved her, and it would have been the truth. Now I don't picture anything."

"I hope you don't think you need to be ashamed around me, Jim."

His face twists in fury as he lifts his gaze. He's scarlet. She is registering that she will never see this man again. "*Ashamed?* I'm not in love with you. Leave me alone. At least Nell and I—we're working at marriage. You're the queen of loneliness. You and Rob—what a joke."

She parks by the lapping water, the shoreline by the wharf, because her eyes—it happens without warning— have blurred; the periphery is edged amber. Her eyeballs actually ache. It's part of the secret life of surgery, the aftereffects that no one else can see. Marriage as work, work, work—when had people quit talking about men and women in terms of joy that made their hearts stop?

Her optometrist has given her an exercise called convergence stimulation for when her eyes seize up and refuse to function together. She takes a piece of paper from the glove compartment. It's already marked with two sets of concentric circles, horizontally side by side. She holds the paper at arm's length while resting a pencil between the sets of circles and moves the pencil toward herself, focusing on the point but staying aware of the circles.

A third set of circles appears, wavering in the middle. This invented set is three-dimensional, shaped like a cup.

She relaxes her focus, glances away, and looks back. She's supposed to be able to summon back that ghost image, that floating imaginary cup, just from wanting it to be there. This time the phantom refuses to show. The paper won't quit shaking.

Grant's, the restaurant run by the blind, has barely opened—five o'clock—when Maria finds it. Black paper covers the windows, cutting off the view of the Bay on one side and the rest of the buildings in the Fort Mason complex on the other. There's a dramatic drop to the temperature, a pulling at the flesh. Maria knots her shawl at her breastbone; she didn't bring a flashlight, did not imagine, foolishly enough, that it would be dark inside. She reattaches the butterfly in her hair, which will glow—a small bit of cheer, though not enough to undo the dragon-like squalor with Nell and Jim. She's oddly brightly colored in her pink, green, and white.

Most of the other reporters haven't arrived, but she recognizes the man sitting on a low wall, watching her. Benedikt Dvořák looks like someone playing the part of a dark-haired doctor from war-torn Europe, deepened into smoldering kindness through some past grief. Except that he's the real thing. He's from Eastern Europe. He's a doctor. He comes over and says, "You're here for the same reason I'm here," and offers his hand. She takes it. "I can tell."

They stand outside the entrance, and Maria says, "Good, I was terrified I'd be on my own." He blocks the sunlight so that she's free to grin at him without shielding her eyes, and when her shawl slips, he adjusts it back on her shoulder.

A blind woman in a blue paisley dress emerges through the hanging strips of dark felt that block the light at the entranceway. She sensed their arrival. Maria mentions her assignment from the *Chronicle* and also that she is lucky to have Dr. Benedikt Dvořák with her, and the woman says, "Oh, my. Oh, yes, Doctor. I heard you on the television. Welcome. Thank you for writing about what it's like to be always inside the night."

He replies that it is his pleasure, she is very kind. His accent is slight but definite enough for him to convey that language requires his good-natured vigilance.

The hostess in the blue dress asks him to put his hand on the back of her shoulder, and tells Maria to put her hand on Benedikt's shoulder. She guides them, attached, through three layers of hanging felt. The complete darkness of the interior does not even permit those specks of white or red light that sighted people store inside their eyelids.

It takes them a while to seat themselves—knees, elbows, trunks—at a wooden table. Benedikt has faster night vision and reports a lack of lighting fixtures and décor. The tables are long, very plain. The woman explains that only one meal is cooked a night. Since there's time before the other writers arrive, they might wish to meet the chef, Grant Blakely.

Slowly, with the same confusion of arms and legs, they extract themselves from the table, and Benedikt puts his hand on the woman's shoulder again and Maria holds onto his, and they are led into the pitch-black kitchen. The woman in blue says, "Grant? Dr. Benedikt Dvořák is here, and a lady from the *Chronicle*," and the chef says, "Sir? Where are you?" Benedikt steps in the direction of the voice; Grant touches his face. "I want to know what you look like. I've read your articles in Braille," he says. He reaches toward Maria. "Hello, lady from the *Chronicle*." He runs his fingertips over her neck and face, pausing to stroke the pearls hanging from her ears. She's not sure what to do. She rests her fingertips on this stranger's face, his aquiline nose and thick skin. An assistant feels around until he finds her arm and runs a hand down to her hand and places a flashlight in it. "You'll want to see how we cook," he says.

The full moon of light that she moves around the kitchen reveals the men, in patches, and one stares with whitened eyes at her, because he can detect the slight heat from the flashlight. Maria turns the beam on Benedikt to amuse him. He makes a face as if he's a criminal caught in some act.

Maria can hear that drinks are being poured, and she says, "Oh, no, I'm supposed to be working."

Benedikt hands her a glass and says, "Then write about how this tastes."

It's champagne. She's tippling with the blind. Grant tells about going out one evening for some milk, and a carload of teenagers threw acid at his face and blinded him. He couldn't keep up with the pace, and the strain of generous tolerance, at the restaurant where he worked. He is fifty-five and has been a chef for only eight years. He'd given up a career as a lawyer for something that gave him actual pleasure.

He wife read about a restaurant in Amsterdam staffed by the blind, with a months-long waiting list, and that is how Grant's came into being. He worries; his place is slower than most San Franciscans can stand, and he's teetering on the brink of ruin. Maria watches a cook measuring broth by pouring it into a bowl and touching the center to figure out its height. Everything that comes out of here must have the taste of their hands.

Benedikt puts his arm around Maria to locate her glass and pours her more champagne.

They are led back to their table. A few more people have come in. Voices instinctively lower. The air feels soft but thick, a swaddling material. In the dark, she can sense that Benedikt must need to shave often, that the hair is already emerging on his face, and she looks at the side of his nose where she recalls, from her earlier glance, that he has a faint scar. What else does she recall from their brief meeting outside? His eyes slant downward toward his temples, where there's silver hair, and his eyes are brown. He seems unruffled by their not speaking, but since he's European surely he can advise intelligently about Madrid, should she go abroad for a year, and that involves branching into a discussion about Rob, and separation, and delays, and Nell's outburst—she stops. Why is she blathering like a schoolgirl?

He understands her dilemma: His own wife took a job in Washington, D.C., and they have been apart for two years but are now trying to put everything together. He has recently disentangled himself from an affair with someone else, one of those mad forays when both the man and the woman agree to get divorces and start over and suddenly the bottom falls out. He thinks it's about time to head back home, and his wife has agreed to meet him there and find a new job. He means Boston, but Maria sees the gray but shining vision of Prague, and says, "What's it like, your home? When I hear about Prague, I see Kafka. And neat, fattening pastries, and you look through a clean glass-plate shop window at them on trays. Probably you want to say, 'You left out the tanks in the street.'"

He's fifty-two; he remembers the tanks. "But the pictures you have aren't wrong. They're the parts of Prague that show. I grew up in a closet-sized apartment, and we turned the faucet on with a wrench, and my mother drank so much vodka she had spots of black blood under her skin and her eyes had coats of varnish. But I took care of her anyway, and she described to me the lions she saw crawling on the wallpaper when she was drunk, but it was all of it mine and needing to get away didn't mean I didn't love it very much."

She says it's a sad story, but she likes his telling of it.

"I should take you to Prague," he says.

"This is so strange, isn't it? That I'm talking to you but I can't really see you at all. As if talking to you means I'm talking to myself."

"Except that I'm here," he says.

140

The waitress feels her way along the edges of the tables and brings them a bottle of cabernet, Stags' Leap. Other reporters have filtered in, collected in a hush. They must eat carefully and put their glasses down without hurry, and she and Benedikt joke about maybe having to feed each other. The menu this evening is trout, whole, with bread stuffing and a sauce of tomatoes and olives. There's an escarole salad with oranges. Green beans fried in batter called "Little Fish from the Garden." The plates come out one by one with an agonizing but elaborate slowness. Maria is jolted; she perceives the scent of the food in color. "I can smell the oranges as orange," she reports to Benedikt, "and the tomatoes as redness, and the salad as green."

He says, "That's what the brain does, sweetheart, it tells the eye what it already knows is true, and the eye says, All right, I'll see it even if it isn't visible this moment. I'll *put* it there for all the other senses to enjoy."

She's read Dvořák's articles—about the colorblind army pilot hired to detect camouflage, the girl who sees only the bottom half of the world, the man who can't control his eyelids, the Palomino girl who sees fly specks over objects, the boy who draws ghosts—but the stories are mostly about their eating, working, talking, and yearning, how they move through their day. "The people you and Oliver Sacks write about are—slightly off," she says. "How they move around is made new because of their ailment, but it's the familiar world."

"Their condition. The oddity that's their good fortune." He adds that El Greco didn't paint elongated people to be arty. That was the true recording of how his eyes saw things.

Europeans—Maria suspects they believe it, too—often seem like religion, history, and ancient buildings finely chopped into forcemeat that's fitted into their skins, enabling them to talk about the universe without sounding self-important.

Like most reserved women, she's a liner-up of anecdotes; she goes to events with a jewel box of ones preselected from the same color end of the spectrum and plucks them out, so she conjures a memory of going to a synagogue for the deaf with her first husband, where her father-in-law had been a cantor for the hearing while a choir of deaf people in robes swayed and signed the lyrics with their hands, a wave of cobalt-blue satin, of arms and fingers, answered by a click-click harmony made by the deaf congregation, signing back as their way of singing along.

"Write that down," Benedikt says. "It's beautiful when people use a different one of their senses and more than make up for something they lack."

When he puts his hand on her arm and asks why she's quavering, she says it must be because of Nell and Jim. "Our friendship perished a while ago, but today we buried it," she says. He quotes Gertrude Stein's warning: "Before the flowers of friendship fade, friendship fades."

"But I didn't realize she hated me," says Maria. "We used to get along. I guess. She wiped all that out, too, my memories of us getting along."

"Hate you? Why? You seem perfectly lovely to me."

"I think it's because I don't want to die," she says, and excuses herself. She needs to use the toilet and the waitress must conduct her there. She's reminded of her surgery, when she needed help in the hospital. The waitress says, still in a nurse's role, "You holler out now, honey, if you need me, and don't you worry, I've been around the naked stuff plenty of times."

The soap in the dispenser has such a strong scent of roses that she's hit with a profusion of them, red, orange, yellow, fire colors. She sees herself as a girl with her Argentine grandmother, who taught her that sticking a rose's thorns under her fingernails and offering the pain to God would make God merciful.

She has to be led back to the table, and Benedikt stands to steady her into place. "When I was in Catholic school," she says, "we weren't allowed to use the bathroom on the first Thursday of every month—"

"Confession day. Right before First Friday."

"You, too? You have the same grim past? So we'd sit there thinking, Okay, I haven't wet the floor yet, I can last another minute. And then another minute, and another, and you get through an hour, and suddenly—disaster. To this day, I can't leave the house without using the bathroom for fear I'll be caught like that, ready to explode. It's a syndrome called Catholic bladder. I failed once in second grade. I had to stand in the hallway in my wet skirt, holding the picture of a crying baby."

"We never got punished like that," he says. "Just laughed at."

"What got to me was that the picture had been carefully matted by one of the nuns. A pretty red border. A neat glue job."

A waitress feels her way over and asks if the whispers are true that Dr. Benedikt Dvořák is here. May she tell him her story?

He gropes in the dark and puts his hand over hers, outstretched toward him, and says, "Yes."

She sits down. "I'm twenty-two, and I lived like a prisoner with my mother. I'd be seeing some boy, and she'd yell: *You will never see him again!* Always that: *You will never see him again!* My mother was crazy. She'd go to bed alone and sob. The days kept going by like that, all the same."

"Poor darling," says Benedikt.

She rests her head against him and says, "It took courage for me to come to you. I haven't been touched since then."

"I won't forget you," he says. "Stay a moment, if you like."

But she has to tend to her customers, and their own waitress brings the bill. Payment is on the honor system, since no one can count the money. Maria says it's on her tab, or rather the newspaper's. Benedikt says no, he's been in the realms of the blind before but he's never known anything like tonight, he's full, drunk, and quite happy.

He pays the bill and says, "Did you bring a car? I'll take a cab. I'm staying at the Fairmont."

She chatters on about the Fairmont being where the U.N. Charter was signed, and in the days of ladies' white gloves, the change got washed, quarters and dimes, so that no one had to handle dirty money. This, he assents, is all complete news to him. She tries a clumsy joke about laundered money and becomes frantic for a new subject. "Do you know Oliver Sacks?" she says.

"Yes," he says. "We go swimming together."

She's startled; it seems so relaxed, so workaday. "I'll give you a lift, but do you mind driving? I mean, pardon my foolishness, but do you want us both to live? I've had some drinks and I'm not the best driver to begin with and—do you mind?"

He agrees that he is very much looking forward to living through the night, and as they step outside, it's surprisingly bright still, and rounds of silver attack Maria's eyes. As a child one Christmas, passing the aluminum tree, she was bombarded by dizzying circles that seemed to attach to the sparkle of the cat's-eye corners of her glasses. They've raced forward to join her where she is right now. She has to close her eyes to keep them from watering, and he holds her face on both sides with his hands, and says, "It's a shock, the light. Keep them closed." His breath brushes her face. When she opens her eyes, he's staring right into them, and she's stunned; not even her own husband has ever looked right into her like this. "I'm dying," she says.

"Nothing bad is happening to you," he says. "You're safe."

"I'm dying to—I'd like to know if you wouldn't mind kissing me."

She means later, when they are hidden, but he pulls her against him and she's kissing wildly out before God and man. When he lifts his mouth away, she gasps as if she can't get enough air. "Where shall I take you?" he asks.

"Anywhere," she says. "It has to be right now. Take me anyplace."

Baby. Sweetheart. She's forty-two, but a lover has never uttered that at her. *Am I crushing you? Do I weigh too much?* The blood is pounding in her face, her stomach and thighs; the blood in his erection is warm in her hand, *Crush me, go ahead.* Curious that she's never been with an

145

uncircumcised man before. The nightstand at the Fairmont glows black; they keep the lamps low. She's soaked an outline of herself onto the bed sheets. She sits for a long time impaled on his lap and they rock together. *Sweetheart, Benedikt, when did you first want me?* (When has she called someone that before?) His tongue traces the outline of her ear. *When you first turned to me. When I was sitting minding my own business on the wall. Out in the light before I knew your name.* She wants to ask if it is always like this for him. She's dripping wet and swollen and releases a raw sound that she's sure suggests a wounded animal, but she also suspects that should he recall her later on, should he play tonight back in his mind as one of those discrete surprises that can exist if one goes out to seize it, he will, most likely, file it as the cry of someone who is always like this, who longs for this so much that she manages to find it, threading all those sweet nothings back inside herself whenever she so wants them.

She's astonished when he calls her three days later. He's back in town, some promotion for an anthology he's in, and walking with her arm linked in his in the night, slowly up Lyon Street, pausing when they're out of breath on the hills to take in the view, a dangerous little rhythm gets released in her head: *I'm going to have him again, I have him again, him here with me in the night.* He takes her to the Steinhardt Aquarium at noon, and it is the extension of night into daylight that makes her hold onto him in the center of Golden Gate Park, her tongue aimed at the back of his throat, his hand down the front of her sweater, being seen, not letting him go.

Then, following the way of these things, nothing; silence. Except that she has, insanely, a vision of him

146

escorting her to a concert in Lincoln Center. (What are they seeing? Why are they in New York? Is it winter? Is that why she's painted a picture of herself in a white scarf and him in a black one?) While trying on a dress, a short one with spaghetti straps and sequined blue roses, a silly incantation alights in her ear: *I should take you to Prague.*

She goes to work, she sees Robert on the weekends; *should, could, I shall take you to Prague.* The new dress can be worn to dinners in Prague, while he whispers the translations of what's being said. *You're safe.* He takes her to see the apartment building where he grew up, where he's never returned. In a room with a canopied bed, he says, *Say it, say you need me to fuck you.* She goes out to dine alone in San Francisco, her face strained in brave bewilderment. She orders wine, dessert, pretends to be reading a book; she flees. There is a shameful recess in women's minds, where childish thoughts are nursed, held like infants who demand their owners' lives. It is a terrible error to imagine that something designed as a moment could be forced into a turning point. He'd mentioned a wife, and getting over someone else. He'd told the blind woman he'd remember her. He creates pockets, alveoli, of intricate existence, pleats within the hours. He feasts upon moments, and with her, he'd in fact extended the time to more than she'd expected. It was a simple love affair, not even that, a moment longer than a moment, highly delineated, permanent and singular but small, if only she'd allow that. And yet. And yet—it has cracked her open. *Here, love, is St. Vitus Cathedral, with its underground tombs of Czech kings; it took nearly six centuries to build. Let's find my room and forget the city.*

147

Maria gains ten pounds and loses them: Now what was the meaning of that? Her days consist of segments of self-inflicted homework. Her ear is avid for tales of a man and a woman not seeing each other for years and then happening upon each other. She is nothing but a skin over common foolishness, aware, ceaselessly, that it is how one handles the end or moves on or doesn't, how one stores it, ignores it, uses it furiously one way or another to get on with things, that makes the difference between dwindling toward death or not. Who wants to be Madame Butterfly; that's a lifetime commitment.

One day, paging through a magazine, she sees his article on the restaurant of the blind. She makes a cameo appearance as "a friend and colleague," which, she tells herself, she is. The photo of Dr. Benedikt Dvořák and his wife, Victoria, a playwright and theater producer, is set in their house, spacious, lined with books, with Italian marionettes on a shelf. All of this is only the natural and predictable result of nearly everything.

The piece gets included in his new collection that stays a long time on the bestsellers list. Her story about that night, (she, Miss Valor and Discretion, hadn't mentioned him), consigned to a Sunday supplement of the *Chronicle*, had been cut in two. For the usual reasons of space, her editor had explained. It ends up on the web, where it garners 215 views.

She agrees with Rob that they've long been separated in idea and now should state as much in deed. She accepts the appointment for a year at the news bureau in Madrid in an attempt at utter change.

A friend in whom Maria confides says, If you found what you want with this doctor fellow, that's a sign that more is out there, you'll find it again. And it's his life's excellence that you want as much as him.

But alone in her bed-sitter, in the premier city that's traded day for night, Maria spots the crucial error in her plan to plaster time over her erotic wound. Just any random act that appears forward-moving will not work, and one runs out of patience with things that can be classified as a learning experience.

She picks up a man in a bar and discovers that Nell—who sent her a birthday card that Maria will not answer—is entirely wrong. Men are quite distinguishable in the dark. *I should take you to Prague*: How on earth has that refrain pursued her here? *Would you like to visit the Prague Sun, the obscene monstrance with its six thousand diamonds, or shall I run my mouth over your stomach?*

It's after the man who's provided some by-the-book pummeling is dressing, saying, American girl she like the dick, and after the owner of the bed-sitter refuses to make Maria any more espresso, having decided she's a whore, that she recalls an incident years ago with Robert, during a fire in Laguna Beach when they were on vacation. He'd gone with a friend on a motor scooter to "size up the damage," leaving her in what he called "the safety of her room" at the hotel. On the television she viewed the fire in a single orange track halving a hillside, like a surgical line of stitching. The fear was that the wind could shift its course at any moment. Ashes were thick not four blocks from the hotel. Rob burst in, carrying kiwi lime wine coolers, so nauseatingly sweet that the sight of them made her sick. He never drank that sort of swill. He'd been close to the flames. Exhilarated by the disaster. He'd seen a house go up and was eager to get out there again, you know, sort of a reporter.

When he reached out to make love to her, she'd recoiled. It's only now that she matches this with something else: That's exactly how she had been when covering the earthquake in the Marina.

There's much to absorb here: The Prado. *Sweetheart, baby.* The work at the bureau is about as weighty as a feather. She can take a train to Barcelona, stand before the marvels of Gaudí. *You love that, don't you.* She's heard that you have to squint in the sunshine at his famous cathedral and tilt back your head to take it all in, this monument that he spent a lifetime pointing into the sky, hoping never to finish, that the stone creatures and jewels in their boxes and niches will dazzle you blind, for when on earth will you see this ever again, this place that explodes the very notion of the ordinary, the functional, the unimposing; the undressed and undone?

Utter

We killed puffins for a living. Barefoot men scaled the cliffs of our island of St. Kilda, and the murders were awful because the birds had impossibly thick necks. It was left to us women to boil them into a glue that stayed stringy when we ate it.

We burned peat inside our cold homes until the walls were black and so were the tiny windows where the smoky faces of our neighbors tried to peek in, and I screamed at John that I had to visit the mainland or I would stop breathing.

And because visiting Edinburgh took all the extra we had, this was my punishment: I met a woman I liked at once while lining up with John for our tour bus in front of McBride's Tea Shoppe off King's Road. She and I were laughing like girls when her husband joined us, and the worst possible thing happened. I loved him on sight, utterly—and there's a word I'd not used before nor have I used since. I could not look at him. After the castle with the eleventh-century cannonball stuck in the wall, as I sat next to John, with this woman and my true love in the seat ahead of us on the bus, I stared at the fish-hook curl of hair at the back of his neck. Once I did reach out and touch it while pretending that his label was sticking out. He said, "Thank you, love." In the line for tickets at the Museum of Gaelic Weapons, he stood next to me inhaling strangely full, and with a start I realized: The same miracle has happened to him.

I cried to John that I had to run to America or I would expire. We spent everything left to smuggle ourselves across the sea and then through Canada. At a shop in Michigan, my new home, I found Easter eggs frosted with yellows and pinks that convinced me that Americans will never have any idea how hopeful they are. When I looked into the peephole of the Easter egg, I saw tiny chicks and a little farmhouse with a red heart on its roof, and I began to weep with such a joy that I told John I must learn to drive or my insides would collapse, and I think he said, "Good, let them." Because I had been distant, but who would not be with the way he was always coming home at night in a rage about this or that union quarrel, and he's right, I didn't care then and never shall I.

I drove our Ford (John the eternal optimist says that stands for "Found on Road Dead") fast through the pine forests of Michigan until they marbled green. I stopped for apples, they're like heads bloated with the color of shame, at a roadside stand, and all at once my veins in a riot I kept going, across the border.

I developed a wee unearthly taste for a sweet I found in a French shop in Windsor. They called it their "Isadora Duncan," a sponge soaked in what kind of spirits I could not tell. But there was more. I had never seen anything where instead of stopping at richness, more richness is added. They split the cake and smeared it with a dark, seeded jam, and on the top they put candied violets in a bouquet. Like the bouquets they must have given the grand actress as she bowed night after lovely night. How brave she was, Isadora, going on with the show even when she had that wooden leg!

I could not stay away from Windsor. Isadora was waving me toward her, saying, Come, Addy. These violets have your name on them.

But back home, the divine taste left me writhing on my bed, clutching my midsection, and John said, "Addy, we don't have permission to be in this country, and you don't have a license to drive. Keep crossing the border like that and at last I'll be done with you."

The next day I risked deportation again by driving across the border because Isadora was full inside me, and forever after that oh it was wonderful how much I could do without at home, saving up, so that I could eat nothing else.

But it got so I was thinking I was as good with talk as Isadora, with her diamonds and her sharp speeches, and I answered John back and he pushed me into a wall. I was lying down, arms and legs wide, with the room tilting me here and there, with him saying, "I'm sorry, Addy, but will you come home to me now?"

The French lady at the shop has loved getting to know me, and we chat about Isadora. I didn't know that the actress died in a car. I didn't know that the wind caught her dramatic long scarf and tied it around the tailpipe so that she strangled to death. The air must have invisible hands that touched her all over but then tied a silk noose.

This makes me cry so. I own such a sadness to learn how she drove herself to an end. Because I'm aiming very hard to picture her alive and shouting into the floodlights,

I've managed to crash myself into this ditch by the side of the road. I've hurt my leg. I haven't the courage to let beauty and speed take me in one grip out of the world, as Isadora did, but I will have a crutch to pretend that I'm her with a wooden leg.

I couldn't make it out of Windsor, so when the ambulance comes I imagine the immigration police will also be here, though now my stomach aches so to double me over. I wonder if John will come to my rescue from the Michigan side, or maybe he'll yell, "You dashed our refuge with your going across the border day after day." I'll offer him the Isadora Duncan I keep for my trip home, and he'll hesitate, his angry face like a splat of flesh, long enough for me to stuff it furiously into myself.

But probably I won't hear a thing at all, because I've gone so far I cainna hear nothing but my driving heart, and when they peek through the glass of my driver's window, they'll see me straining to get into reverse because this day is already running round to meet the next and the time is already upon me to race back for more.

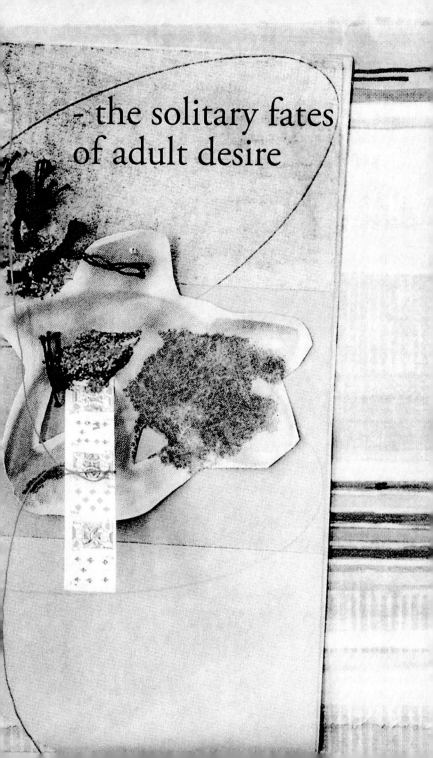

- the solitary fates
of adult desire

Fig. 6 (BACK). *I made yet another home of pretty things with pretty things stored within.*

The Love Life of an Assistant Animator

A naked woman got hidden inside every film. Nathan Porter knew that, everyone knew that. The animators would slip one drawing into every episode, and the speed of the film made her disappear. She was there but not there. Spreading her legs or holding her bare breasts—the animators got bored and it was their fun. Maybe children watching their Saturday morning cartoons were getting dirty pictures imprinted on their brains. But soon enough everyone gets to carry around desires so deep that often he doesn't know he's having them.

Did anyone ever die in your arms? That was a question often put to Nathan after Vietnam. People needed to look at someone who had looked at that. They wanted to paint a few scenes and run them together, to enjoy the shudder at a distance, coloring in the details at their leisure—the jungle one hundred shades of green. *Did you kill any babies? Did you have to duck?* He was six-five. Six feet by the time he was thirteen in Michigan, lying under the piano while his mother played sonatas, like George Sand listening to Chopin. Nathan was growing so fast his bones hurt if he stood too long. He'd eat a quart of strawberry ice cream at a time but the pink film barely soothed him, and once he'd screamed because he hadn't asked to be skin and bones and hunger. It was sexual in a way he couldn't define when people said, *Tell me what it was like,* and their eyes widened. He was one of the lucky ones, he said. Built like a jackknife, his eye level higher than most, onto one of the first helicopters out of Saigon. No one had died in his arms. He never connected the bullets he fired to the sound of a man falling. He would never tell anyone about the girl in the sand. He would not let people bury her in the starring role, the best part of the movie they were begging Nathan to insert into their heads. That had always distinguished him: a far-reaching code on the subject of betrayal.

He also possessed a disturbing aptitude for patience. Nathan suspected that it came from an inability to accept certain truths, a belief that if he only waited long enough the world would see the wisdom of what he wanted and some dovetailing of fate would bring it to him. At the University of Michigan, he had perched in a tree for five hours to win a keg of beer for his dormitory. He once did sketches of a nude woman for twenty consecutive hours, after the rest of the class had left, because he had to capture her perfectly and the model wanted to be caught perfectly, and he fell a bit in love to discover that her ability to fix herself and not move matched his own.

That was how he ended up after the war, at age twenty-three, as an assistant animator at the Delmar Studios in West Los Angeles. The work required drawing skills and maniacal patience. Nathan's Uncle Sid, in story development at Disney's, called East Lansing with news about the job; everyone wanted to pry Nathan out of his dark, childhood bedroom with its Wolverine pennants.

Union wages. Benefits. California's fried white sunshine.
Nathan couldn't admit that he wanted to be a famous
artist, and assistant animation seemed a suitable bluff. One
more night of his mother making him Ovaltine and he
would sob worse than the time that his Jack Russell terrier,
Dorothy, had run under the wheels of a car before he
could save her.

Delmar Studios, a low-lying, yellow building, was on
Pico Boulevard and bore the spray paint of the Sotel 13
gang pushing west and the Santa Monica 13 gang going
east. Before the janitor painted yellow again over the
letters, Nathan could size up who was winning the night
wars. Yellow over black over red—the toxic skins were
piling up. The studio was one of the lesser ones, with one
minor cartoon series and one hit called "The Hive," about
bees that solved animal crimes.

Nathan perched at his light-board in a small room with
Jen and Barbara, the other assistant animators. The lights
stabbed brightness through their eyes and burned into
their skulls. Nathan would do his time and instead of
coveting a promotion to animator, he'd try for character
development, the highest-paying job. Then he would quit
and paint for the rest of his life. His patience wasn't dutiful
so much as calculating. He had ambition. There was no
point in having spellbinding patience unless it was
attached to a leap ahead.

He hardly spoke to the women flanking him. Barbara
was a collector of slights, real and imagined, and her flesh
expanded to contain them. Jen had dots for eyes, a round
head, thin lips, and short brown hair with bangs, like a
child's drawing of a woman. They both enjoyed disliking
their husbands and then did all they could to impart to

Nathan that he could not claim to be a true adult until he drank deeply from the cup of marital bliss. Every afternoon at four, Jen's daughter called to report that she was home from school, and Jen chanted, "I love you, Mathilda. Did you hear me? I said, 'I love you, Mathilda.' What do *you* say? Remember our talk? *I love you.* What? Louder, dear."

When Nathan closed his eyes, his parents were still waving farewell to him through their double-paned windows. The Remington bronco rested on the cherry-wood table. At the vanishing point while driving away, he turned and a jolt of realism almost undid him, to see them reduced to small figures under glass, contained in a paperweight. In his mind, the house shook and covered them with a flurry of gold glitter.

An animator would draw: *Jen looking at phone. Then: Jen talking into phone.* The assistants were the in-between-ers. They drew each incremental stage between the main poses, tilting the tracing paper to go a fraction farther into the action, ten steps of the phone closing in on an ear. A mouth redrawn ten times in the spaces between "I-L-o-v-e-Y-o-u." Replicating life at its slowest speed. Honoring every nuance of motion. Spending days on the wings of flying bees. The cell-painters recreated each step in color. When speeded up, the cells blurred into continuous action. Answer the phone, I love you.

Nathan defrosting enchiladas at his apartment on Kiowa off of Bundy. Nathan alone in bed. Thousands of steps in between, drinking a beer with *I love you* ringing in his ears, jogging on San Vicente Boulevard, I love you, love, love, Nathan at his Uncle Sid's in Pasadena, a ship-shape Arts & Crafts model home, enduring stories from World War

II, the last true war with a real enemy, Nathan hurrying away, not trading stories of his own. He must protect the girl in the sand. Nathan at home, painting irises in oils and throwing them away; after Van Gogh, who can dare a purple flower? Vincent was loved by his brother, but it did not save him. No one loves you enough, Mathilda, and I like you for knowing it.

Nathan meeting a woman. Nathan at their parting. An average of three thousand animated steps per day and still the film misses half the beats.

The glaring, unmoving sky made him sneeze. *You're allergic to the sun,* said Becky, a girl with a black mini-dress and green sunglasses. He met her in line at the Westward Ho Market. A scratcher in bed. A three-week affair. Affair? Collision. *Fucking A, the sun hates you, Nathan, how can you stand your bad luck?*

One morning at work, a high voice entered him, right through his skin. It was coming from someone unseen, in the hallway. He had the odd but not disagreeable sensation of something familiar that he could not name. It was a shock that he first took for pain and then realized was pleasure; it hurts when the clay cracks off a man who's been dead. Right away he felt he was wrong; the sound was high, but it was low, too. The voice had everything at once—but not in a jumble. Articulated. He surrendered. Who could describe it?

The music of it was so generous that it also lit up Jen and Barbara. Jen said, "Oh, good. I guess Mrs. Delmar has come back."

Violet Delmar owned a prize voice. She'd narrated an opera series for television and got called in to do wildlife programs, Disney heroines. Her voice-over for a Tide commercial was said to earn her eighty thousand a year from residuals. She had already been streaming into Nathan's head for years. Journalists tried to capture her tone with overused words—"silk," say—but silk was silk, and Violet was Violet. It was reasonable to think that Norman Delmar had taken money out of his wife's voice to open his animation studio.

Nathan first saw her inside the sound booth, recording tracks for some female roles in the cartoons. She was in her late thirties, and although she wasn't heavy, she had hips that no amount of exercise would reduce. Though this was utterly foreign to him, he found himself not unmoved by such a predicament. Her red hair seemed prematurely thin. She had on a white blouse and a denim skirt that hit mid-calf but that a woman could unbutton up the middle as high as she liked, and Mrs. Delmar undid hers to slightly above the knee. Her stockings had vivid designs.

Nathan was among the employees who arranged their coffee breaks to listen to Mrs. Delmar. She usually came in at ten in the morning to do her recordings. There were Sam Edelson, an animator, a cell-painter named Lisa, and Liz from Accounting. Nathan had a mild crush on Liz, who was forty-eight but was still wearing white lipstick and dyeing her hair jet-black. He was fixated upon the beauty mark near her left eye. He commented about the high and low of Violet's voice, and Liz grabbed his arm and said, "That's it! Every word's got top notes and bottom notes. Like a perfume does."

Notes, perfume—their connection was a mystery to him.

One time Violet finished early and emerged from the booth, and Sam broke into applause. Violet blushed rather horribly. Nathan accepted this as the condition of people who are not quite beautiful. They are particularly shy when reminded that they are stuck forever in their own skins. Her earrings were orange fish, like garibaldis. She caught Nathan's eye, as if the woman who was a famous voice needed help in knowing what to say. He blurted, "Where does it come from?"

What did he mean? Star power? Her voice? Getting paid for being purely who you were, because of some innate quality?

She appeared grateful and touched the front of her neck. He wasn't sure how she understood what he had asked, since he didn't know himself. "My mother sang me very nice lullabies," she said. "Maybe they got stuck in my throat instead of my head."

She was awkward at even this type of minor parting, and said, "Goodbye, my lovelies," the sign-off from "The Hive." She put on a sun hat with cherries, the kind on sale at seaside resorts.

When he climbed back into his chair to resume work, Barbara said, "Isn't Liz married, Nathan?"

He stared at her. "To a nice man. As you already know."

"I was just wondering if you did."

"I didn't know it was against the law to speak to married women, Barb."

"She probably just needed help ratting her black helmet," said Jen.

"Liz is terrific," he said, loudly. "I like her."

They looked pale and boiled as they stared down at the lights and traced such precise stages of larks in descent that

163

they seemed to be gunning them down in slow motion. He would never comprehend why it made him such an unusual breed, to resist attacking a friend. To refuse joining the mob in feasting. *Why are the fish hurting that one, Dad? It's sick, Nathan. We'll remove it so it can die in peace.* He loathed anyone who could savage you behind your back and then look you in the eye. Part of this was virtuous of him, but most of it wasn't. He hated trying to guess what was going on inside someone, what someone really thought of him. Jen could be cruel about Liz's hair and then go have tea with her, and nothing would seem like betrayal. Jen and Barbara would age right here and dissolve into X-rays while the Sotel 13 and SM 13 armies battled through the night.

His chance to escape arrived with the news from Liz that the studio was about to close contracts for two new shows. "A Rare Bird" and some space-age thing. Barry Wills was the inventor of characters but would need to hire one new person, maybe two. Nathan had drawn a portrait of Liz that she had tacked up in Accounting, and she would never speak to him again if he did not apply for the job. "Hurry up and get famous, Nathan," she said. "I want to sell your picture of me and retire from this dump."

He handed his portfolio to Barry Wills on the same day that Violet Delmar stopped coming in to record voice-overs. She was out auditioning for movies, and it was not unpleasing to think of her taking the next step upward in a sort of parallel ascension to his own. The question remained whether she would, with her shyness, cross over from being a hidden star—in lesser avenues—to a visible presence. "Good luck, Mrs. Delmar, and good luck to me," he announced while standing at his sink, eating a fried-tomato sandwich.

Barry Wills kept him waiting. Days of pretending not to see Nathan strolling by his office. Wills had a room to himself, where he read scripts and dreamed up creatures that got stuck into the memories of children.

Nathan went to the planetarium ("Why Mars Looks Like Fire"), and met a medical student, Jasmine, who laughed about her parking tickets and moving violations. Was this a good thing, he asked, for a future doctor to collect moving violations? Didn't that imply harm? *It implies speed, that's all.* She asked about the medics in Vietnam. He said tape, glue, hacksaws, screaming, what did he know. *What* do *you know, Nathan? Do you like drawing bees and fish?* She called him "tall and handsome" so that it sounded like a species. They were eating trout and drinking cabernet in a place with a tin ceiling to collect and crush the din and pack it into ears. He excused himself and stood at a urinal in the men's room, trying to figure out his dismay. He was having dinner with a pretty girl who would go back to his place with him. Glancing at the other men, he had it: He could send any of them to sit in his place, and Jasmine would not notice. He could be anyone sufficiently good-looking and sexually alert and "interesting" in his work. The right thing to do would be to climb out the bathroom's window, but he saw Jasmine for a while before they moved on.

It took three weeks before Barry Wills left a note for Nathan to come talk to him. Wills worked at a draftsman's table with his back to the door. After a lengthy minute of waiting to be noticed, Nathan said, "Mr. Wills?" The room was a startling red with white trim and gave the appearance of welcoming you inside lean meat. Awards and sketches of Barry's famous characters were in gold frames.

Nathan's brief career as an assistant animator had already alerted him to the infinitesimal steps within a single motion, and his pulse adjusted itself to the exact cadence with which Barry Wills put down a pencil, straightened, and turned from his drawing board. He looked unsure as to why Nathan was in the building, much less filling his doorframe.

"You asked me to come and see you, Mr. Wills."

"I thought you were Jewish. What kind of a Jewish name is Porter?"

"It started out as Tannenbaum, sir." He cringed. Sir? "My grandfather thought it would be more American to name himself after his job."

"Hotels?"

"No. He was a porter on Amtrak."

"A white man?"

"Well, yes. I suppose so." On an animation board, this entire minute would be discarded as action spun in the wrong direction, a miscue of calibration. "With the new contracts coming in, you'll need—"

"Right, Porter, you can help me carry my burden." He located Nathan's portfolio in a stack of papers and opened it. Cartoon birds, safari animals. Nathan had included a sketch, done in red crayon, from his marathon session in college, which Wills held up. "This isn't bad, Nathan. As a sketch. As a woman, she's fat and red. What exactly am I supposed to do with it?"

"I wanted to show you what I can do, I guess, Mr. Wills."

"To show you're better than what gets done here."

"That's not what I meant."

"Sure it is. You probably are better than what gets done here, Nathan."

Wills took a marking pen and redid a sketch. "A vulture with a garland?" He changed the garland into spikes. "Cute is Disney. Cute is out, Nathan."

"Okay." He didn't think the vulture was cute in the way that Barry meant. The script named the vulture Daisy, and Nathan had thrown a garland over her head. A touch literal. He had things to learn. Barry deflated the round bodies of the remaining animals and then stuffed them along with the red nude back into the portfolio so that it looked like a badly made sandwich and slung everything onto a cabinet.

Absurdity dropped Nathan into something close to wonder. He had seen the fall of Saigon, and Barry had survived Normandy, and they were discussing birds with garlands. A man could rise up from where he stood, but that hardly meant he had planted himself in the right place. But at the moment Nathan had no idea what to do except move forward from where he now was. "Will I have a chance, Mr. Wills? To work with you?"

Barry trained his watery blue eyes on Nathan. "I'd say you have a good chance, Mr. Porter."

Nathan returned to his light-board, blinking with surprise. He fell into the rhythm of presenting Barry Wills with sketches, waiting for a week, making an inquiry, receiving revisions. Barry would not give him a definite no or yes about moving up; he insisted that Nathan tend to the artwork and not worry. Liz once looked at his revisions and said, "Gosh, Nathan, what do I know? Mr. Wills must be right. But I liked your first version better."

Sometimes Barry Wills treated Nathan to his revision lessons in the animators' room, so that Christian Harvey, Jim Thornley, and Rob Klein could witness Nathan's schooling. The place had the feel of an elephants' graveyard, though Nathan liked Sam Edelson, a quiet man caving into slow-moving alcoholism, five, six shots a day so that he didn't feel hardcore but got to kill himself by inches. He was preferable to Jason Ridley, a twenty-eight-year-old who wore childlike train engineer's hats and was already aware that his brilliance would never convert to anything outside of cartoons. One afternoon, while Nathan watched Barry redo one of his drawings, Jason said, "Have you heard? No one wants the boss's wife."

Violet's auditions were not going well. She had read for ten film roles and drawn blank after blank. What blasted open was like a strange, howling sound chamber filling with jibes from Christian, Jim, Bob, Barry, and Jason. Imagine the Famous Voice presuming it could speak as a Famous Actress. At least in the sound booth her legs stayed invisible. That huge ass, in a romantic lead? That face?

The outpouring transpired with a breathtaking speed, faster than Sam or Nathan could form words to stop it, and it was right then that Norman Delmar stepped into the room. The silence that passed over them was still saturated with taunts. Nathan had never experienced this sharply that words could stay drifting in the air, attaching everywhere like dust.

168

"Norm," said Jason. "Esteemed boss-man. We were just wondering when Violet's going to be a star."

Norman glanced around, at their faces. His eyes were light gray when you glanced at him, but a deep gray when you looked right into him. He was average height but had the bearing of a coiled spring. Nathan could see the calculations clicking inside Norman's head. He had missed the cracks about his wife, but suspected that things had been said that should not go unanswered; he also had to make light of things they hadn't intended for him to hear, or there would have to be a tiring, low-level war. What he said, mildly, was, "Hey, she'll strike it rich if she knows what's good for her."

Nathan said, "What a thing to say about your wife."

Norman's face tightened, but they were all distracted to see a person striding by the doorway, no more than a flash of her.

Nathan went into the hallway and saw Mrs. Delmar in her hat with the cherries, hurrying away. He wasn't sure if she'd heard only him, or nothing, or the entire exchange. She couldn't have heard the stupid insults; her husband came in afterward and would have seen her standing there.

"Mrs. Delmar?"

She stood but did not turn around, like a child told to wait. Nathan had to walk around to the front of her. Her skin was a liability. She couldn't hide inside it. Her whole body was scarlet. She took off her hat as if she had a sudden inkling that people saw her as ridiculous, and she said, "Yes?"

"I just want to ask if you're okay, Mrs. Delmar." He took the hat from her grip and put it on her head. "It looks nice on you," he said.

"Vi?" It was Norm coming up the hallway, but not very fast.

"What does 'okay' mean, Nathan? Men and their 'okays.'" Everyone in America knew that voice as detached, but he knew it as attached to someone.

"Men aren't okay. You are. I hope," he said.

She smiled. There was a gap between her top front teeth, and her eyes were shining. She put the fingertips of one hand on his chest and said, "You are too, I hope." It was like an echo with three sides to it, a dimension to sound that he'd never heard before. A voice had come from inside him, and he had given it to her, and she was giving it back to him, but not before she'd restrung the tones with a low joy and high sadness.

Norman arrived. "Dear?" he said. She was silent but took his arm, and Nathan drove home and drank enough Guinness to blacken his bones.

When he was called to Norman Delmar's office, he wondered briefly if Barry Wills had finally, after months of torture, decided to elevate him to an inventor of characters for "A Rare Bird." It was one shard of a thought, no more or less real than what actually occurred, which was for Norman Delmar to open his mahogany entertainment center and run the film for a new episode of "The Hive." He hit the stop-action button and pointed. Imbedded in the film, invisible at full-speed, was Nathan's red nude.

"That your work, Nathan?"

"It's my drawing," he said, "but I didn't put it there."

"You think this is funny, smart guy?"

"You know the guys—do this. Worse, usually."

"Worse? So making fun of my wife is fucking okay?"

Nathan had a falling sensation, like those animated moments when an animal goes off the cliff and stops with false hope in mid-air. "I don't know why you think that's your wife, Mr. Delmar. I did that in college."

A heavy redhead. Large hips. A round face. *That's my wife.* Good enough. Norman needed a reason not to look at Nathan anymore after Nathan had shamed him, and here it was. Norman Delmar and not some Jew boy would be defending Violet from now on. Nathan took his severance check and walked past Barry Wills' office. Barry had his back to him. Nathan paused—what could he say? Why did you do that to my sketch? He had no idea who had brought it to Mr. Delmar's attention, but that didn't matter. Mr. Delmar was going to be looking for something, and it had been handed to him sooner rather than later.

Liz burst into tears when he kissed her goodbye, and even Barbara and Jen seemed stricken. Sam Edelson said, "You're better than here anyway, Nathan," and Nathan said, "Take care of yourself, Sam," and that was all. He stole a stapler and some pencils. He contemplated phoning Jasmine, but he was haloed with the scent of failure and she would wrinkle her nose.

Lying on his bed, drinking beer, losing track of the hours, he listened to the phone machine broadcast his Uncle Sid's voice, *Whadja do? Something about a naked woman? They're even laughing about it at Disney's. For Christ's sake, I get you a job, and you screw up. Look, get over here so Beth can feed you. Hey, kid? You okay?*

Men and their okays.

He sat at his easel, painting women in their daily lives—naked. Naked women buying oranges in the market. Naked women kissing cartoon figures. Naked women weeping while the clothed family ate a turkey. His brush stopped mid-air when pealing over the phone machine, and filling his small rooms, was the voice of Violet Delmar. "Nathan? I would like you to have lunch with me." His first thought was that Norman Delmar got to wake up every morning and hear those sounds. His second thought broke down into a grief that was muscular: If Uncle Sid had heard the story, probably Violet had as well. She might think that Nathan had been making fun of her.

When he met Mrs. Delmar at Michael's, an outdoor café in Pacific Palisades, the ocean was motionless and the wind had died. The décor was blue and white. It had been so long since Nathan had entered such a composed scene that it felt wrong. Mrs. Delmar, already pink from the sun, was in a white blouse and navy skirt, with stockings decorated with palm trees.

She stood when she saw him and grinned. She didn't seem angry with him. He did not want to eat a hamburger in front of Mrs. Delmar, but he could not think of what he wanted. "I'll have what you've having," he said.

"You may not want that, Nathan," she said. "I get the consommé." She patted her midsection. "I'm reading for parts. I have to compete with girls who look half my age. Some of them *are* half my age."

"You look fine, Mrs. Delmar." He had no idea what consommé was. His mother had used cans of Campbell's beef consommé to make gravy.

"How old are you, Nathan? Do you mind my asking?"

"I'm almost twenty-four."

"I'm thirty-eight. Guess what happens. My agent gets me a reading, and I confirm it by phone, and they say, 'Oh, wait—you're—wait, don't tell me. You're very familiar.' But when they walk into the reception area, they keep looking around, and I say, 'I'm Violet,' and their faces fall. Like this." She did four or five faces for Nathan. "They say, 'Your voice doesn't match you.'"

"How can your voice not match you? I mean—it's your voice."

They laughed. "Well, yes, it seems that way to me, too, Nathan."

Mrs. Delmar asked a waitress in a polo shirt and shorts for two orders of the Consommé Aurore and two glasses of chardonnay. The waitress stared and then thought better of asking Mrs. Delmar who she was.

So this was what it was like, going places when you were famous but not quite. People heard her as they might stumble across a memory only a little beyond their grasp. She must hear it constantly: *Oh, haven't we met—?* He knew she'd say, *Why, yes.* Because, in a sense, she'd entered their ears at some point to stay for good. Days might go by before the answer came: *Yes, it was the famous American Voice, I should've asked how she herself would describe it. But why describe a song instead of singing it? Why describe a person who is right outside a door instead of opening the door?*

She said it was all a bit unreal, because she had wanted to be an opera singer. "I had the size, the projection, you have to be born with that," she said.

He said that wanting to be an opera singer was a good dream.

"The problem is that you can't be good. Or excellent. You have to be world-class outstanding. I have a pretty voice, I know that, but I have no idea what I can match it to that means something."

He voiced his sympathy for the man with the tenth-best record in the hundred-yard dash in the Olympics. He took off his jacket and muttered that he wanted to be an artist, and he went into shock. His buried secret, never uttered to anyone, had been given to a woman whose husband had fired him. It was a relief that the wine and soup arrived. Two filaments of white meat floated in a brown soup tinged red. How did she live on this stuff?

"What I mean is that I know what it's like to be good at something but not good enough," he said.

"You're more than good, Nathan. I saw the—I heard about the—oh, dear." She put down her spoon, and he put down his. She stretched her arm toward him, belly-side up. He saw the blue veins, the strings that attached to other strings to make up her vocal cords. "Nathan? That—picture. You shouldn't have put it in one of the children's—"

"Mrs. Delmar, I don't know what you heard, but—"

"Nathan, was that woman really supposed to be me?"

"Mrs. Delmar," he said, "God, no. God!"

She tasted her consommé. "This is very nice, Nathan. Try it."

"Why did you think it was you? That I would do that. To you." What infernal heat in California. Sweat spilled from under his arms to stain his shirt a wet dark blue. The top of her bent head showed patches of scalp, and he had an impulse to knock over this bowl of fancy beige water and kiss the bareness and ask if he could put his tongue in the space between her front teeth.

"Because I'm a silly woman," she said. "I thought it was—you know, hidden. For me."

He drank half his wine, and it instantly flowed into his head. He set his glass down and looked at her. She seemed ready to cry.

"Then it was," he said. "Sure, Mrs. Delmar." A Valentine not available to the naked eye. "Why not," he said. He got her to look up.

The consommé surprised him. It had one taste but also several others. He'd thought of tastes as single items. Mrs. Delmar explained that this was the beauty of something simple, that it contained the work of immense clarification, the richest part cooked out of the marrow, the glistening that came from knowing how to whip in egg whites that collected the sediments and got strained out. The word didn't come from "consumer" for consuming, the way many people thought—Nathan had never thought of it at all, he assured her—but from "consommer," to consummate, since it was the summing up of the essence out of bones, this pure complicated simple thing.

She asked him about Vietnam, and he almost told her about the girl in the sand, but he didn't, and her gaze read clear through to his troubles. She was the smartest woman he had ever met, much smarter than barrel-ahead Norman. Nathan could not bear that she might have overheard anything in the animators' room. "Mrs. Delmar, did you hear? What we said. You know. Me. Your husband." He regretted his stupidity; Mrs. Delmar's face trembled.

"It's Violet. You can call me by name."

"I don't know what got into me. Violet. Forget what I said."

"But that's just it, Nathan. I can't ever forget things. I don't know what Norm said. I heard you saying what you did. So Norm had to have said something sort of bad. About me. Right? You've seen through me. I thought, I'll have lunch with Nathan, and somehow without putting him on the spot, it'll come out. There. I've said it. Now you won't think much of me."

"Listen, Violet, I don't blame you for wanting to know, but it's better to ignore things like that. Norman's a nice guy."

"Is he? It's funny. Someone who's supposed to be close to me said something awful, and I should ask him but I can't."

He watched her fighting the divide from her husband: She'd have to decide whether to forgive him, or if this discovery would undo everything.

"The least I can do is not let them take your job away," she said. "That's another reason I wanted to talk to you."

"Never mind about that. I learned a lot from Mr. Wills."

"You sure did. I heard he was redoing your sketches. If you were that terrible, wouldn't he have told you to get lost?"

Nathan sat back in his chair. His ideas about Wills had been vague—something to do with letting Nathan know that getting into the club meant going through a wringer. But it had not been clear until right now, words matched up correctly to nuances, that Wills had not tormented him because he had no talent, but because he did. Barry wasn't going to let some boy saunter in and outdraw him. And he seized his chance to do Nathan in. He'd be almost grateful to Wills for this primal lesson if he were not also stuck with no idea of what to do next.

"I appreciate everything you've been saying, Mrs. Delmar. I really do," he said. "I should have seen it coming. The ambush, I mean."

She insisted on paying the check. "You'll call me," she said, "if you want my help? With finding work?"

He said that being fired was for the best. He shuddered. He was turning into the typical American, convinced that when doors slammed shut, magical ones opened that guaranteed an ever-brighter future.

He walked her to the parking garage, but when they reached her car, she turned to him and thrust her head against his chest and began to cry. Her voice twisted into a sob that started from some far place inside her, and she kept her face buried against him.

"Mrs. Delmar?" he said. He put his arms around her.

"I'm embarrassing myself. I'm acting like a fat weepy old fool."

"You're nowhere near being a fool, Violet," he said. "You're nothing but wonderful."

She stood back from him and smiled, and his hands were huge enough for him to put them on either side of her face and use the thumbs to clear the tears away. She had green eyes.

"Goodbye, Nathan," she said. "I'll go home now."

Home. Time to go home. "Me, too," he said. "Goodbye, Violet."

Nathan got a job as a mail carrier, since it allowed him to wander the streets with a clarified purpose. He guessed at the lives of people on his route without reading postcards or looking too closely at letters, since that

st Prices Paid for Hides and
ARENDTSVILLE, PA

Katherine
Vaz

FIG. 7. *You stepped into my arms in the Final Act, and I hold on still.*

seemed a violation of a trust. He received a letter of his own, from Mrs. Delmar.

Dear Nathan,

You bring me good luck. Not long after our lunch, I got a part in a movie. I'm to be a raging alcoholic, the kind of role that starlets take when they're forty, and everyone thinks they're brave for being raw. So—raw I shall be. Norman seems pleased on my behalf. I hope you'll forgive me some day for troubling you with my woes. I know that awaiting you is much success and happiness.

Fondly,
Violet

Nathan asleep alone in bed. Nathan discovering the difficulty of painting something complex that is at the same time clear and simple. Maybe he was an animator as early as his boyhood, every time he sprinted, commanding the pines of Michigan to become a blur. The edges of them bleeding, concealing the owls and reducing a fox to a dot of fire. Maybe he was learning even then that he was the one running and running, but it was the place that was flowing fast away from him. Maybe that red sketch really was Mrs. Delmar. Before he met her, he was dreaming her up, sitting there hour after hour trying to get her just right. Already he was dashing through bursts that said *love, love, lily-of-the-valley* whenever his mother sprayed her blue atomizer and he'd dash through the cloud of the air changed, and he thought, *She pressed a button and out came perfume that stays in a cloud,* and only later could he animate the connection, that a past action can linger and become more itself in the present, actual particles of sweeter air. Followed by a million in-between steps until he learned that perfume has properties called top notes and bottom notes, that these were waiting in the blue atomizer all along, though he knew nothing about it at the time. His grandpa took Nathan on train rides and pointed through the window as the wheels rocked them almost to sleep, *There they are, the Great Plains, the forests, Nathan, the white clouds like hats for the mountains, the lakes, the invisible borders, I want to guard it all, I love trains because they carry me over the land*, with Nathan as the guardian of the terrain of his grandpa's face; in the dining car, he brushed crumbs from his grandpa's white mustache. His eyes are my lakes, his skin my country. *Don't look down, Nathan, if the motion makes you sick; eyes up, straight ahead, at the horizon.*

Except that keeping a head up can get it blown off. But Nathan lifts his eyes from books about Vietnam when the grunts are too street-wise; maybe it was just his luck to be in a company of boys who probably also came from the edges of pine forests, carrying pictures from their senior prom as they stared down, looking for trip-wires. No army buddy died in his arms. He was looking at the horizon and was not the first to see the girl in the sand. Sergeant Whitcomb had pulled her from a tree, a Viet Cong girl with a rifle, maybe sixteen, and he had her black hair in his fist. Nathan hadn't heard her rifle. She'd missed someone's head, Lopez's, maybe, because he kept running his hand over his skull and saying, Christ. He'd felt the heat of a bullet, as close a layer as it gets without furrowing open your scalp. Lopez wanted nothing to do with her, and he and Nathan were the ones, when the Sergeant ripped off her black trousers and started going at her, who were saying, No, don't, and then it was someone else's turn to rape her, but it was on a bed of sand, and her head was going under. *It's better when they're dying*, said someone, *the cunt goes into spasms.* Just the girl's pussy in the air and her head below the sand, making the sand move. Lopez and Nathan were the ones pulling someone off her, and Nathan pulled her head out of the sand. She said some words he didn't understand, but that didn't matter. The voice is true and clearest when it's the body speaking. Her face was free and her crotch and nostrils were bleeding. *Speak. Speak. Speak.* She looked right at Nathan and said some word that he tried without luck to have translated when he went home, her breath did some indecipherable refiguring of the air, it might have been saying thanks or cussing at him for ninety seconds more of life, because right then Whitcomb said, *Porter, I don't want to shoot you so I'm going to have to shoot her, you dumb cocksucker*, and he rammed his AK-47 at her vagina and blew off her head. She didn't die in Nathan's arms. She had her last minute of life in his arms, and then it was Lopez screeching and vomiting, and Nathan cleaning him up. Two weeks later, the length of an American vacation, he was home, away from something so far out of the narrative sync of his life that he did not understand why a scene that removed should now become the central bottom wailing note to everything he would be condemned to do.

He stopped wandering the streets with the mail during the invention of Claymation. He did well with a short feature, "My Troubled Year," that he co-wrote with someone who'd been fired from a different cartoon studio. No one could believe how Claymation worked. You manipulated a clay figure a hair's breath of an action forward—it was like assistant animation, except in a third dimension—and you shot film, and then you moved the clay again, maybe against a new clay landscape, shot film, and edited the million frames so that your hands and every trace of you were removed and the time speeded up. It took forever. People thought it was magic because no one could believe that anyone would have a patience close to insanity. Nathan adored it: He was invisible, but lifeless clay was suddenly walking and speaking, arms and legs going like mad. Their film was about a housepainter who falls in love with a Gloria-Swanson-type actress, a sort of Little Tramp meets Sunset Boulevard. The colors he paints her dark manor revive her. In the final frame, he kisses her and they both turn bright red, as if their kiss is spilling over to cover their bodies, their insides taking over their outsides.

He and his co-author won an Oscar for "Best Animated Feature."

Nominated that year for Best Actress—though she did not win—was Violet Delmar for her role as a hard-drinking, pill-popping loner, a portrait so at variance with his memory of her that he called ten "Delmar, N."s in the phone book until he got her voice, which made him hang up.

She must have forgiven the old dunderhead. Norman seemed less knowable to Nathan than the clay figures that went warm from his continual handling of them. Violet was a famous voice looking for proper vessels, and Norman was the one with plans for it, Norman the well-ruddered force, his cartoon studio a mere step toward owning a studio that made movies with real people, not animated ones. Nathan knew that his reduction of the

Delmars couldn't be entirely true. Anyone that Violet could stay with had to have, imbedded in him, some persistence of affection. That scene in the animators' room could be slipped into a long-running marriage as a flicker that vanished, swallowed up by the far view. Making it into a mature, un-Nathan kind of love.

Nathan married Doreen O'Malley six weeks after meeting her. She was hired to design a look for some Claymation figures in his next film, and at first he resisted but then had to admit that she fleshed out inanimate clay better than he could on his own. He liked her. She was his age, slender, and her tennis shoes had those dangling balls at the heels that made him think of a dog's gonads. She exploded his adolescent image of Catholic girls with their knees together, mumbling prayers; she was a smoker, drinker, and fierce kisser. He had his worries: She could eat minestrone for a week and then curl her lip at it. After working on a screenplay fifteen hours a day for two weeks, she put it away, never to be spoken of again. He took this as a personal warning. She might be too much in the mold of a classic volleyball player to love with complete comfort, and as a costume designer she was not so much dressed as outfitted. But she was also staggeringly beautiful, a throaty singer. Doreen went to bed with him after their second date and didn't seem to fall in love as much as prove she could swallow him whole, if she wanted. He decided that would suit him fine.

The speed of the years would have taken his breath away if he had stopped to notice, though at some point, in the general fast-forward of his married life, a diagnostic backward glance confirmed that he and Doreen were on schedule. The surmountable lull in affections arrived right when their twin boys did. The affairs that he and Doreen managed were few and slight, designed as secret scenes played out quickly, off the main track, though a day came when he figured that Doreen was in love with someone with no plans to take her from him, because he found her crying and when he put his hand on her shoulder she did not shrug it off. It seemed the position of someone very young, who had not yet spent sustained time with anyone, to imagine that closeness always arose from proximity, that what someone actually thought of you was one collapsible, portable revelation away.

Galleries in Los Angeles and San Francisco sold his drawings and paintings, including some of his old nudes. A solo show at the Corcoran in Washington led to some galleries in New York, and he acquired a minor following. "You're B-team," Doreen said, "but impressively B-Team, Nathan." It was cruel, except that Doreen was more vicious about her own small victories in costume design, and one day she simply quit and announced that it was time for her to start "being" instead of "doing." She would go in reverse. This meant that Nathan would need to *be* less and *do* more himself.

He took the leap to sculpture, chunky Rodin-knock-offs that Doreen did not like until *The Los Angeles Times* wrote a good review. At the Kryker Gallery, filled with Nathan's statues of naked men and women, he saw a girl with acne, and the world froze. He was back to being a teenager—this girl was walking around with his body, the days of him wearing his anxiety on his face, his insides boiling, every hour an agony of waiting to outgrow it. Doreen looked at her, too, and whispered to Nathan, "I'd kill myself." A variegated chill pierced him. He had married his enemy.

He followed the gentle rise in the fortunes of Violet Delmar, the brief coverage in the movie magazines and Calendar section of the *Times*. She had done well in two more movies but remained on the fringes. And then one Sunday, he opened the paper and saw a photo of her at a premiere, on the arm of a young actor. The caption read: "Seen around town: Ed Kincaid with the woman who will always be The Voice." She looked worn but happy, not a bad way to forge ahead, to appealing exhaustion. Away from old Norm.

He received a postcard with crowded writing:

Nathan!

I bought a painting of yours here in New York! Norman's rare-bird show did well. He's producing movies now. We're divorced-but-friends. I've given up guessing what's next; they keep wanting me to play blowsy lost women, and I keep saying no. To try for other things, I've lost weight, which is a torment—a torment—but no "other things" appear. I know you're very very busy.

You've done animation, and you've done sculpture. Have you thought of kinetic sculpture? You'd be perfect.

Love & the rest of it,
Violet

He was haunted by her underlining of "a torment," and by the doubling of the word "very," and he kept backing over the image of her at a desk, writing those high-nerved things. What was "the rest of it"? He had no idea how to reply and kept the postcard in his jeans until

Doreen threw them in the wash and the card got pounded down to its fibers.

He thought of flying to New York, punching out the Kincaid guy, and making life-detonating love to this woman he scarcely knew, after a speech about living to the point of ruin, since everyone got ruined anyway. Instead, he buried his father; he applauded his boys, Kyle and Jeff, when they graduated from high school; he moved his mother to a care home when she sank into dementia. Instead of getting butter for her bread, she did this: Stood. Walked to refrigerator. Opened door. Forgot why she was there. Remembered. Picked up the butter, and so on, until he wondered why she didn't scream.

One evening, on his way to meet Doreen at Le Louve, a restaurant in Westwood, he got caught in traffic so thick at the cross of Barrington and San Vicente that he had time to step from the driver's seat. A bicycle ahead on the sidewalk made him abandon his car and run to the scene, where the man who had hit the cyclist was saying, "The ambulance is on its way. I've called. Okay? I've called." Nathan looked at the man and at the Latino fellow with blood streaming from his mouth and asked, "*¿Habla inglés?*" and when the cyclist flailed, Nathan said, "I'll keep talking, save your breath, but don't shut your eyes, I'm not a doctor, but whatever you do, don't fall asleep." Around them rose what Nathan thought of as the L. A. symphony, a helix of the sounds of horns, furious leanings, and when the cyclist stopped breathing, Nathan sealed his mouth to the mouth of the dying man. He'd learned CPR in the army. The sun beat down and Nathan looked up and breathed into him again, and when the cyclist's lungs inflated, he smiled weakly at Nathan, and Nathan would never figure out what possessed him to say, "*Soy un padre.*" He was grateful to Doreen. Otherwise he would not have learned about absolution, about wanting to be forgiven for your entire life when your final minute arrived. Nathan used his terrible Spanish to indicate that he'd left his clerical collar elsewhere. The cyclist almost grinned. He knew that Nathan was not a priest. The ambulance arrived and took the cyclist away. The driver talked to the police, and when Nathan was free to return to his car, nosed to the side of the road, he sat behind the wheel, weeping with horror and relief. The man's blood was on the front of his shirt. But no one had died in his arms.

Doreen was later than he was to the restaurant, and when she plunked down, she said, "There was an accident. Fucking mess. Then I saw glass and police and I thought, *finally*. Now everything can lighten up." She saw the blood on his shirt, but he said he'd had a nosebleed.

That's what Californians did: voice relief when they came across an accident, because it meant that now their own progress would be clear. He'd done it himself any number of times. The mystery of not-moving was met; the cars could flow on. You could wait for years, but eventually an essence of a place would show, the leakage out of its bones. This would become California for him. He refused to eat for days, even after calling the hospital and hearing that the victim had survived. When he confessed the truth to Doreen, she argued that this was an ordinary city story, and the man had lived, and Nathan should get over it. "But it's *my* ordinary story," he said. "A man was going to die. He bled on me. He didn't know the language. It's my fucking *ordinary* story, and it's *his*, and it's the story of this entire *non-fucking* place."

His first kinetic sculpture consisted of men tied up by their wheeled feet, their heads on a revolving platform as blood flowed out and got recycled back into them. A tape recorder played yells, shouts, screams. Doreen informed him that he was sick, but the sculpture ended up in the Museum of Modern Art in New York. *Life Magazine* took a photo and mentioned that artist Nathan Porter insisted upon using animal blood from slaughterhouses, and "City Limits" was a fine entry into the school of noisy art with a real voice. When Doreen said she was proud, he felt worse than if she'd followed through and left him. Her marriage counseling consisted of the assent of others.

He saw pictures of Violet with a new boyfriend in Paris; he read mixed reviews of her in a new movie, which ended up precipitating a decline for her, right as his own fortunes as a kinetic sculptor rose.

He received a postcard:

Dear Nathan,

I saw your shockingly beautiful work in *Life*. I admired the screech in it. You gladden my aging days. I saw a picture of you and Doreen in some society page; I'm forgetting where. I hate forgetting so much! Now I've run out of time and money, and back to L.A. I take my worn-out hide.

Love,
Violet

He wrote a letter back, using the address of the hotel, the Esmeralda in the Latin Quarter:

The Love Life of an Assistant Animator

Dear Violet,

That "shockingly beautiful" move came from you. Mostly I have no idea what to do next. I'm happy to hear you're coming home. I am sorry for not tracking your whereabouts to say that your movies have been nothing but wonderful, though they make me worry about you. This means you are good in what you have done.

Love,
Nathan

It was returned "Addressee Unknown." She had already vanished.

On Nathan's twentieth wedding anniversary, he surprised Doreen with a weekend in San Francisco. Her daily routine now consisted of drinking steadily from five in the afternoon until falling asleep at midnight, and when they were trying to have a quiet argument about her ordering a second champagne in the War Memorial Opera House before taking their seats for *La Traviata*, he heard, "Nathan? Is this really you?"

He had heard her voice at regular intervals on film, he had seen her in the newspaper and movies, but he had not seen her in the flesh for two decades. He took a moment before turning to her, playing it out a measure or two, the different sound of her actual voice. She would now be about fifty-nine. He moved arm, body, eyes. Violet Delmar was standing against the railing near the bar, holding a tumbler of sparkling water. Time had gone a desirable way with her. Her red hair was thicker, and she looked healthy but she still had those heavy hips, and she wore a sapphire ring instead of a wedding band. He walked closer, with Doreen following him. She had even closed the gap between her front teeth. He wished she hadn't. But he admired that instead of being in black eveningwear like everyone else within eyesight and earshot, she was in a beaded rose-colored gown that ended in a fishtail. He stammered, "Are you here by yourself?"

"Why, I believe I am. But you know that saying, don't you? 'Sometimes the best company is being alone.'"

"I do," said Nathan. "I know that saying."

Violet shook Doreen's hand and said, "This is a wonderful surprise."

"Yes," said Doreen. "Who are you? I recognize your voice."

"She's done movies, since the voice," said Nathan.

"What?" said Doreen.

Violet laughed. "I have the same old voice, it's just moved around a bit, that's all. Never mind. None of that matters."

"We're here for our twentieth anniversary," said Doreen.

"Then congratulations," she said. "You've outdone me. Norm and I still talk, but we only managed nineteen years. Shall I buy you a drink?"

"No," said Nathan.

"Yes," said Doreen. "He's no fun, but I'm lots of fun."

Doreen downed a whisky, and he and Violet had clear, plain water, and in the minutes before the bell to call them to their seats, Doreen's conversation with Violet washed over him as if he were underwater and the words roared on the liquid surface: Queries and answers, all about Norman doing car-crash movies while Violet did "dark small pictures," and then Doreen's drunken exhortations about "being versus doing," and right as the bell sounded, Nathan said, "It's torment. You wrote that to me. About torment. You look great."

Violet stopped and touched his face. Her green eyes turned large and wet. The great American voice took a startling leap, because there was no sound, no sentence spoken aloud. Just the reverberating of her insides, going through her hand and into his skin.

She turned without a word and left them.

When the opera was over, Nathan could not find Violet to say goodbye. In the car, Doreen mimicked Violet's voice, though she was nowhere near hitting any of its tones. "You've outdone me, Nathan."

"What?" he said. "What was that for?"

"It's not as if I think you're pure as the driven snow, Nathan. You can't just say, Gee, it was good to see one of my old girlfriends. Or new ones, or whatever she is. But I guess in this case *old* would be the word, but now I'm being mean but I can't stop myself. She seemed lonely. Fuck."

"Fuck what?" he said. "She isn't a girlfriend, and she wasn't one in the past." What was he doing, testifying before a Senate subcommittee? "I've never slept with that woman, Dorrie, but she's a good friend," he said, though this, too, struck a note that was perfectly true and curiously wrong.

"You don't sleep with me either, Nathan!"

She went crazy. He almost crashed the car. So little between them had anything approaching vehemence that her fury stunned him. The outpouring continued at the hotel through the night and into the morning, *Torment, what was that about?* Because Doreen knew herself what

191

torment was, and he replied that her torment was that she needed more to *do*, that she did nothing all day anymore and it had taken her voice away from her, and she screamed that that's what *he* had done, with his fucking embarrassing grotesque statues dripping blood, and he said he thought she was proud of all the notice he'd received, and she said that he made assumptions because he was so *stupid* about women, as for one little example he imagined they wanted to be *saved*, and he said, "*I'd* like to be saved," and she yelled, "Then join Jews for Jesus," and on and on, until she was hoarse and couldn't speak and they both lay on the bed, holding hands, having finally reached a simultaneous splicing of themselves, as every married man and woman managed sooner or later, at that juncture of wondering if it showed strength of character to soldier on with the choices made, to submit to the long promises littered with difficulties and unhappiness, or if strength of character meant admitting a rupture was beyond repair. A picture of a little sailboat was over the bed.

Nathan having a brief encounter in which he felt love. Nathan alone in bed. In between: The pretty stranger below him, naked, running her hands over his bare arms, crying, with him saying, Did I hurt you? I didn't mean to hurt you. With her touching his hand as he cleared the hair and tears from her face while she murmured, *I picked you across the gallery, it's my fault, because I had the feeling you'd go somewhere with me. I wasn't wrong, was I?*

No, she wasn't wrong.

Everything is more *for me right now. More sad. More happy. My husband got killed three years ago in a plane crash, and I picked you across the gallery to bring me back to life.*

I'm sorry to get teary. I hear men hate that. They say, "Oh, no, this one's a weeper."

No, he was sorry she was crying, but that was all right. It was the screamers he didn't like. No one likes the screamers with their fake oh, God, oh, God, I'm dying. Could he see her again? Had he helped her at all?

Yes, he had no idea how much, but she couldn't see him again because she was awake now and that meant she was in agony. *I'm just here with you for a moment. I'm very grateful to be in pain again. The day says, 'Welcome back to dawn,' and the night says, 'Welcome back to midnight.'*

That's very nice, he said. Not the feeling, but the way you put it. The words you used are sweet. Thank you.

Thank you, Mr. Porter.

While he helped her dress, she said, *Tell me how it works. Animation.*

He felt far too far from speech. So he took a sheet of paper from the motel's desk and wrote: This. Is. The. Way. It. Works.

And then: ThisIsTheWayItWorks.

He explained that digital imaging now rendered the task of assistant animation obsolete. What he'd done for a while in his history no longer existed as necessary. Not such a different fate from most people's. He told the pretty stranger about the habit of the animators of hiding naked women, but now the obscene drawings got caught. Her parting words were: *I heard that some artists threw in a beaver shot of the lead cartoon female in a half-real, half-animated movie. They thought it was invisible, but there was hell to pay.*

Nathan in his bathrobe alone; Doreen out without saying where.

Nathan watching an ancient rerun of "A Rare Bird." Rory the Rare Bird had a splat of mustard-colored hair and did oafish things out of gallantry, which made the chorus of raffish sidekicks twitter with an amusement that Nathan would be condemned to hear into dotage. He gave a bleat of anguish that was pointless, since he wasn't within shouting distance of another living being. The *rara avis* was batting his eyelids at a red-breasted, waddling cardinal. Nathan's hair wasn't the color of Rory's, and he didn't wear glasses, but he knew how to read through the thin veil of a story's camouflaging details: There he was, in love with Violet Delmar. It was that clear. Those soused animator bastards had seen his insides and smeared them onto film. Eating shredded wheat on a Saturday morning while wondering how to ask his wife for a divorce, now that their sons were in college, had been planned as a time-waster. And yet suddenly he was thrust into the second half of life, when you are meant to carry a grief that you will be permitted to survive but from which you will not recover. It coincides with the time when it occurs to you that waiting does not always segue into the triumph that everyone agrees should be accorded to patience. That was when Doreen returned home to find him watching cartoons and sobbing, and from then, to the final dissolution of marriage, to being alone in his bed, seemed the work of hardly a minute.

Nathan Porter was to see Violet Delmar exactly one more time in his life. It was two years after his divorce. He was forty-nine, and Violet was sixty-three. It was during a phase of shame for him, when his kinetic sculptures had made him a name and did well but not well enough to pay for everything. He told a friend who owned a catering business that he would help out now and then for extra money.

While working a party in Bel-Air, picking the tooth-picks from the hors d'oeuvres off a lawn—the kind with cellophane frills in red, yellow, and blue—he heard a voice that made him wish the earth could open and swallow him. The voice was calling his name. He was in a monkey suit that he had hoped made him invisible.

She still had a lovely smile. He had not seen it in so long that it put his breath high enough to block the greeting churning in his throat. Her face was radiant enough to soften the mild, normal lines—she did not seem old so much as deepened, but her hands looked troubled by a stiffening and, distressed, he simply took them in his own hands. She was wearing a wedding ring different from the one for Norman, so he managed to say, stupidly, "You've married someone." They both laughed.

"Well, Nathan," she said. "I've thrown myself at you and—"

"Right now? Or that time in the garage. I didn't want to take advantage of you when you seemed unhappy."

"Oh—men and their 'I only want to be happy.' What does that mean, Nathan?" she said, grinning. "Our timing has always been incredibly off. That's all okay, isn't it? Isn't that just our story, yours and mine?"

He touched the side of her face because he hadn't been thinking clearly enough to do it the night in the War Memorial Opera House. He loved how they spoke in echoes, he loved that she didn't even forget the time in the hallway with the business of men and their okays. He wanted to say that she had been so long the underside of his every waking moment that he did not understand why their scenes were so few, with so many years in between. But those scenes had expanded, every second and every gesture of them opened into its own reel, and it was those other times—those other years—that sped up and out of sight.

Speech seemed to exit him by force, but when uttered it barely reached her ear, so that she had to lean her head on his chest. "I really don't see, Mrs. Delmar, how I can go on," he heard himself saying. A man was approaching them, carrying a light coat. That would be her new husband, an older man, coming to collect her and take her toward old age. "What's it like," he said, "to speak and that's enough to be famous and adored, just for being who you are? What's it like, to be beyond words?"

"Not so famous, Nathan. Not so adored."

She was being called away. Her new husband was drawing closer.

Violet Delmar squeezed Nathan's hand. He leaned down and did not quite manage a kiss, just the placement of his face against her face. She put her hand on the back of his neck, where his hairs were standing straight up. "Oh, Nathan," she said. "Whatever will I do, if I think you haven't gone on. Only don't go anywhere just now. Dearest, who can say why, I just know you've always cheered me so immensely."

Sometimes you didn't have to be moving ahead to the next thing, the next scene and minute. Occasionally you could stop. You could stop where you were, stay where it mattered. He wanted to say her name to hear the sound of it in his own voice, but sometimes it was best to give up speaking. Violet Delmar's husband was a stone's throw away, but Nathan quit looking at him. Nathan was too far imbedded in the scene he would imbed within everything for the rest of his days, here in this ill-timed moment, with the surprise of her, with the much-storied woman alive in his arms.

One Must Speak of Sex in French

When the bullet pierces Maddy's knee, she admires her body for the first time in her entire ten years. Because it refuses to feel any pain. For a split second, it feels nothing at all—but as if "nothing" were a lightness, a something, the weight of zero. This will be part of her study on whether heartache is a dot or a string. Her body is insisting, *But I was having such a good time just now.* Others are screaming, wrestling the gun out of stupid little Teddy McPherson's paws, but Maddy is newly, suddenly, desperately at a height of love for her mother, a ballerina who flies in huge arcs, her body made of rope to lasso pure air. Her mother says, *I go past the brink of everyday hurting when I dance.*

But pain, famously, roars when told it isn't wanted. White foam boils out of her mouth. A fresh dull school-yard shooting, Galileo Elementary, babies butchering babies. Yesterday she corrected Teddy McPherson's spelling, so today she must lose a knee. Daddy is a dot. Momma is a string. Momma's feet are de-scaled fish, salmon-fleshed, after *petits jetés, coupés.* Pink ballet shoes exhale Momma's splicing of exhilaration closer, closer, closer to agony. A necklace of barbed stars approaches Maddy's throat. The last thing she registers, as she sinks down to lie in her blood, is Crystal Roma, her very best friend, leaning over her to whisper, *If you stay alive, Maddy, you'll get famous.*

Firebird, Spring

Lillie Roland is engaged in a gentle war with her friend, Bianca Alves. Bianca is a principal dancer with the San Francisco City Ballet; Lillie has managed a few solos, but never a starring role. She does not have many chances left. She is twenty-nine years and two months old. She's been The Blind Girl in "The Miraculous Mandarin" and Hydrola in "Ondine"—but not Ondine. (That was Bianca.) In "Nutcracker," she cheerfully melted into the fluttering cast, dressed in buttercream pastels, her timing sharpened with *esprit de corps*. She felt it like erotic pangs and *it's still there* in her thigh muscles, her longing to be Caroline in "Lilac Garden"; she won a lesser lead.

Tryouts for "Firebird" will be in a few months. She must be the magical bird that wins the kingdom, the golden apples, the lover, and the powers over death.

Aim for inner stillness that's fierce, says Bianca. She stretches at the barre with Lillie, executes a *tour en l'air,* turns back again, breathing hard. *How was I?*

Good, but you can be astonishing. Are you holding back? I don't think so. Am I? Why did you say that?

I'm trying to be honest. Like you are with me. Right?

Birdish tittering laughter. They are trying to remain friends who know they'd surrender friendship to win.

Their arms and legs vanish into a hyperawareness of line. The repetitions appear simple. But repetition that is careless merely irons a lasting mistake into the body.

Lillie executes several pirouettes, and Bianca shouts, *Brava. Where on earth did that come from?*

Lillie is dying to announce that it comes of her learning lately the difference between sex and passion. Yesterday her lover, Mark, stood behind her and tilted her head back *a breath of a second after she fell inside the urge to tilt it back* to stroke the inside of his lower lip with her own, as if all their hours, both solitary and together, were designed toward that perfect reinvention of a kiss.

Mark Galway has entered her often enough to be emerging through her skin. She shines. He is a photographer who won a Pulitzer for capturing some residents of San Diego as they fled a fire. An essay on what people grab when their lives might be over. The photos were taken a while ago but are still reprinted in the international press. He moves in the circles that Lillie touches, edges up to, but doesn't quite travel in. He gives her the joy she needs to be the Firebird.

Instead of mentioning this, she offers a *gracias* to Bianca for the compliment and cools down in silence.

Lillie's husband, Len, teaches kindergarten. Her ballerina friends declare, *I wish I had "a Len."* He shops and cleans and helps Maddy with her homework. But he also says, with a breezy half-laugh, *I have thirty prima donnas in my classroom and two at home.* When Lillie remarks that she's never been an actual prima donna and would love to be one, he says, *Will you be satisfied then?* Len is the one who will fetch the wraps if her friends feel a chill; in private, he says he can't afford to take her to Paris or

Stockholm, places she visited with the company and longs to revisit. Those faraway places do not belong in her head.

I'll die if I'm not the Firebird, Lenny.

Die? Lillie, I've never wanted anything like that. Except you.

Bianca tosses a cashmere sweater perfectly, thoughtlessly, around her shoulders as they prepare to go home. The sunset is vivid and pocked with blots, like an orange stuck with cloves.

Hey, I almost forgot—here's a little gift, she says, handing Lillie a coupon for one of the free killer ice cream dishes at Ghirardelli's.

Lillie takes it, turns it over.

It's not a letter bomb, honey. It's for ice cream, says Bianca, her smile as fixed as a rind. *Don't you love chocolate?*

Thank you. Sabotage can be amusing and tiny. Every ounce of body weight matters now, every minute of straying off the path. Or by chance does Bianca mean to be nice? *Maddy will love it,* says Lillie.

Out near the Cannery, hand in hand with her baby, Lillie Roland's skin is wet with the animal joy of walking. She sips ice water while Maddy orders the Gold Rush Sundae, with walnuts and bittersweet chocolate syrup, at the Ghirardelli Factory. Lillie reaches out and squeezes Maddy's knee. Violence will render her daughter's leg untouchable within a few months, and Maddy will forget how replete she is right now, with a mother who makes time freeze on its grid. They go to Ripley's Believe It Or Not Museum and laugh at the nonsense until a guard starts guffawing, too: *It's so zigzag and shapeless, being alive.*

Her little girl is brilliant and cuts Aztec moons out of thin blue tin. The particulars of Lillie's days occur to her so deeply that they seem connected to life itself, in the abstract-raw.

Her eyes are violet on spotless white. The blood stirred up from Mark's loving of her ebbs back and forth in her breasts.

She sings very loudly in the house, Oh my dahr-LING, oh my dahr-LING, and Maddy bellows, CLEMENTINE . . . and they wait and wait, but Len refuses to answer: *You are lost and gone forever.*

enchaînement

Mark Galway is forty-seven. Today, a Saturday, he is due to meet Lillie at their usual place. While shaving, he gives himself the normal talking-to: He is too old for her, and they are both married, and it must fall to him to be the sage force to bring an end. Their love affair has gone on for six months, and they have crested to a place still shy of reverberating damage. His speech will be brief and kind; he'll hold her as long as he has to. He will miss her habit of planting her open mouth onto his coat or shirt during an embrace; that is both her greeting and her farewell. Several of his jackets retain faint, circular smudges. Her hair is that rare shade that used to be referred to as "apricot."

Odd that something so physical, that has polished away the dull film he was growing over his eyes, should seem so—well, made-up. Who gets to say, *I love a real-live ballerina?*

He drives through the city with its hills; it's one massive, concrete electrocardiogram. In many spots, the cars clot like platelets. They both have keys to the pied-à-terre of a dancer who spends most of the year in New York. It's a one-windowed box at 19th and Sanchez, near Mission Dolores Park, with posters of Paris to add an illusion of air. At first, meeting in such a place had given their adventure a curious, adolescent thrill, but he was surprised at how glad he was at the arrival of domestic touches—crumbs in the sink, underwear with the stains of menstrual blood washed out and left to dry on the towel rack.

His speech about endings slips away; he senses a veering toward the unstoppable: He knocks at the door, rather than letting himself in, because he likes knowing that Lillie will peer through the view hole to see him caught, as she says, "in a drop of water." For a moment, he is reduced to the best of himself, in the stage of about-to-happen, a man aware that a woman is ready to receive him. Trapped under a tiny glass dome, he is a man secretly written upon a day, like the watermark in paper. That is how a love affair, he's decided, imprints itself; it is a translucency within an opacity, mostly invisible but soaked into the fiber, water made permanent.

Lillie opens the door, and he says, Good God.

She is awaiting him naked. He once said she shouldn't bother with clothing; on athletes it's a concession to everyone else's faults. He never imagined she'd give him what he asked for. She is slender and milk-colored with flat breasts; really they're a study in pectoral muscles, nipples painted on as an afterthought. She keeps her pubic hair shaved to near nothing, a slight redness, and— inflaming him—says she'd wax it all off if she didn't fear denuding herself into a girl.

She is in his arms; he holds her hard enough that he fears cracking her bones, but she clutches him that fiercely, too. If they've gone on for six months, seven or eight can't matter terribly. He adores picking her up because she runs her mouth through his hair and he doesn't mind her seeing that the underside is white, under the black waves. Stretching like she's trying to fly sheer over him, she always makes him seem new to her, which makes him seem new to himself. She runs her hard nipple along his lips. *Sweetheart. Lillie.* She has said that hearing her name makes her wild, because like him she's a Catholic, in her case French-Canadian, Sacre Coeur schooling, and she still can never believe that a man is making love to her, and it stuns her into the present when he confirms it by speaking her name. She admits to worshipping what is effortless from him—the faint traces of his accent from his childhood in Belfast, its claim upon another country.

In bed they lie under a sheet decorated with Monet's ponds. *Come inside me, stay inside me.* They seldom flail. It's starkly quiet, a confinement of skin, if a person goes that far into someone else. *You're kissing the hollow of my ankle, what's the name for that?* She rubs her battered feet on his leg—they're torn wrecks, those feet made tender until they're misshapen. He cannot tell her goodbye, not yet.

A fire truck roars past, and they giggle. He calls her "Lillie Coit" after the San Francisco legend who'd been rescued from a fire as a child, though she lost a friend in the disaster. As a socialite, until she died, Coit would leap up from fancy parties to chase after roaring fire engines. Mark and Lillie speak their own language. She says, *Bianca, Firebird,* and he replies, *You'll be the star, the decision is months away*... They have their code regarding punishment, want, repetition, exactitude. In Belfast, the priests tied a rope around a boy's waist and lowered him down the well if he couldn't recite his catechism. One misplaced word got you dangled over the abyss. Lillie taught him "Crim. Com.," an abbreviation that jumped from the dictionary at her: "Criminal Conversation" is a legal term for adultery.

You make me fearless, she says.

Lillie, that comes from you. You've probably always been that way.

Then you make me moreso. *Do you think that's what love is? Bringing out what's best in someone and making it grander so that it's almost scary, and if that person looks down and panics she'll fall?*

You won't fall.

It's the same for you, isn't it? Being grander?

He wants to point out that she's right in some ways and wrong in others. He longs to admit that those fire photos, a decade old, were a grandness that he's lived off of for a while, that he hasn't surpassed them, that they may in fact be the height of his career, and she's mistaken about the glamour she ascribes to him. But this would open the door toward a farther, new intimacy, the one that comes when failings and slippage are allowed to surface, when a person asks to be thought of as who he might be rather than what he has done. She's clutching between his legs and what can he do but say Yes, she makes him bigger than he is, and they use his joke to fall onto each other, and the subject of his fire-people, the sparks in the smoke-filled sky like fireflies batting the faces of the grief-stricken as they pack their limbs into their cars, the girl with the gilded cage and parakeet, the woman carrying a high-school tiara—they're allowed to remain, for a while more, as his inviolate claim to fame. Inexhaustible Lillie, she keeps bringing him back to that time he was young and saw others piercingly, honestly enough to win the prize.

He offers her the usual ride to Judah Street, where she can catch a streetcar home. Home to her husband and child. He remembers he must pick up his laundry, and by surprise—they have seldom done outside things—Lillie says, *I'll go with you, it'll give me another half an hour with you, Mark.*

He is a faithful customer at Mr. Wing's Laundry. (Mark's wife, Rita, says it's racist to go to a Chinese laundry, but Mark says, I don't think Mr. Wing agrees.) Alvin Wing's window display is a solitary junk sailing on a red paper sea, under a red paper sky. Lillie proclaims it lovely; Mark stops to look. Suddenly he can picture Alvin Wing building the model of the junk at a table covered with an unblemished drop cloth, using toothpicks with drops of glue to attach the battened sails. The junk is intricate but clean, its hull perpetually erect, as if it is forging through swells of blood but will reach the shore unbloodied.

Beautiful, beautiful, she says, reaching out to clutch his hand.

He is dumbstruck at the way the air is funneling around her rather than buffeting her and thinks *beautiful, beautiful,* too.

Alvin Wing waits behind the counter. Mark has been here a hundred times but today he follows Lillie's gaze toward the ceiling-high shelves. Ribbons cascade down, controlled explosions. The orders are wrapped in blue gauze that makes the shirts look hospitalized. Mr. Wing's glasses steam up from the heat of being himself; he inclines his head toward a cooler draft, and his glasses clear.

He presents Mark's package as always, gripped with both hands, as if an invisible wonder is being offered on a salver. Mark tends to grab his laundry or tuck it under his arm—a slight lack of rising to occasion, the sort of small failing that can occur frequently without adding up to a failed day.

Lillie says, *I'll take that!* She holds out both hands to receive it. She nods toward the shrine of Longevity Man. *Mr. Wing, next time I'll bring oranges.*

She aligns act and reaction so that even a chore has its dead time removed. He's going to sob with pain. For years he's imagined that it's sexual fireworks he's craved, for years he's found them here and there, when all along it never occurred to him to ask that plain domestic occasions be married to desire. That's what he's been missing.

Blazes. Now. Everything. Love. This. *You.*

The unbinding of the heart that breeds the jaguar below the skin.

Len Chase orders his students to stop taunting Martin, whose pale eyes are faint dots. The poor boy cannot help stuttering. Len helps Martin with artwork, blocks, non-verbal things. During finger-painting, he says, *Martin? Red and blue equal purple! Try mixing those! Good!*

You have a head like a balloon, Marty, someone whispers. *If I punch it, you'll explode.*

Danny, come here and apologize. Right now. A teacher who does not deal with small things instantly will sink below their accumulating weight. He spends his working day stemming the threat of violence. Given half the chance, his kindergarteners would hit, pull hair, humiliate. He never was idealistic about teaching, never a sentimental idiot about the idylls of childhood. He likes being a foot soldier, saving those who can be saved. The honorable rules are that he must coax Martin into the realm of words, but he's an eminent realist. He nurses contempt for colleagues who aspire to sainthood. One day in the lunchroom, when Bette Madison jawed on to the point of tears about how much she loved dedicating her weekends to marking papers, he had to stifle an impulse to stab her with a fork.

As a boy hearing his parents fight, he figured that if he cleaned his room and brought his mother her vodka (watered down, his attempt to cure her while obeying her needs)—all would be well, and it is this "all"—he cannot define it—that keeps him awake at night, with Lillie lying next to him. He married her when she was eighteen and sobbed that she was pregnant by him and her days as a ballerina were over, and he said, *I'll make you see they aren't.*

He'll take care of Lillie; he'll take care of everything. Yesterday it was his turn to wash away the dirty pictures in the boys' bathroom. (*Mr. Pecker says hi, Mr. Chase*—the artistry of the fourth-graders; great, they're only pretending not to know how to spell.) He took pride in how well he deflects the minor impact of such things until he was helping Karen, his prize student, with her reading.

She was grinning, and he said, *Karen?*

Mr. Chase! It's true what Margaret told me, you have that one hair sticking funny out of your mustache.

He laughs it off. But lately when Lillie asks, *How was your day*, he wants to curl up in her lap and say, *Sometimes I hate everyone.* But if he starts that, he will die in the flood of it. So he does not speak. He's afraid, too, that speech will lead to other speeches, and she will confirm that she's having an affair. It's his job to make sure she's happy, but he has not touched her in a year because—why? Lillie insists it's because he's vanished, into the corners of her career, her dilemmas, her parties and invitations, and he tends to scream back, *That's what you demand from me. Who can get a wish in edgewise with your hundreds of needs?*

She bellows, *Then shout louder, Lenny! For God's sake! Tell me what you want!*

In bed, she murmurs far-flung ideas: He can write a bestseller about being an award-winning urban teacher; he can tutor a child who's a "case" and find renown with social scientists; he can assert a secret yearning to travel in Italy, he can—oh, why won't he tell her his dreams?

He pretends at first to be asleep. He can't bring himself to say, Dreams are for morons. I'm content. I wanted to disappear into you, and I've done that. Now that you're finished with me as a support system, you want me to reinvent myself into some dumb grand thing I'm not so we can step into your make-believe notion of The Huge World Platform. What is that, exactly? I've arrived. You're the one who's elsewhere.

Mark finds his wife, Rita, at the table, wrapping Jordan almonds into netting. A friend's daughter is getting married. Mark says, *Is that really necessary?*

Rita hisses, *I guess it isn't,* and with one sweep of her arm knocks everything to the floor. The almonds clatter over the linoleum and look absurd, like a child's remaking of stones. He means, *Do you need to do so much of that yourself?* not *Aren't favors at weddings passé?* He is tempted to tell her that her arm sweep was magnificent. But she is wearing her gray sweat suit and her hair is tied back with a rubber band, and she will assume he is making fun of her.

Mark met Rita when she was pregnant by some married cardiac surgeon. What was he then but a young photographer not long out of Northern Ireland, and he'd said, Sure, he'd marry her and raise the child. It seemed edgy and daring. They would be "complicated," as if life were not forever like that, as if you had to manufacture the excitement of adversity. Mark fell in love with little Edward—now grown and living in Boston. And he did the same with dark-eyed, brown-haired Rita, despite her carrying a torch for this surgeon, though she'd never see him again. But she also seemed sad and clung to Mark and, he figured, would outgrow whatever fantasies ricocheted in her head.

After Edward's birth, Rita said, "I'm hollowed out, so arrange whatever you like, Mark. Just don't leave me." He has not taken advantage of Rita's generous blind eye; his affairs in their twenty-five-year marriage have been brief and delineated, as if they had the barriers at the outset of something undertaken on the road. So he is entirely prepared to step past the obstacle course of the almonds and confess that he will give up his ballerina. He sits down, holds her hand, and asks what's bothering her. Rita has always been quiet, but lately her quietness has deepened toward the silence that desolates first one person and then the other and then any bystanders.

He expects her to say, Arrangements are one thing, but have you fallen in love with someone?

Instead, she bursts into tears and races into the living room to unearth a volume called *Passion Play* (!) written by Dr. Heart Surgeon, who manages his time so immortally that he can write poems nominated this year, this late in the game, for a National Book Award (though he's failed to win the prize, Mark notes with what little satisfaction might be left to him). The book falls open easily to a center page. Rita stabs a finger at it. He is forced to listen to her recite a line: *I buried myself in clawing Rita, so that had to be goodbye.*

The doctor is aware that he has a son with her and yet has contributed not a *sou*, since the prosaic task of an upbringing is better suited to a mick camera jockey. What does this doltish line mean? That the doctor once clawed himself to the inside of Mark's wife, to reside there like a tapeworm? Or that Rita was a clawing, demanding wreck? Or—heavy, ironic doctor—*both*. What is making her weep is how little she mattered. She fans the rest of the book under Mark's eyes and assists him in gleaning that it's a Valentine to the surgeon's wife and to some other woman who is clearly not Rita.

She wants him to say, *There, there, he's a fool,* except that it's Mark who feels like one. *What do you expect me to do, Rita?*

I knew you wouldn't care.

You're damn right I don't. What knocks me out is that you give a shit for an asshole who should have been cleared out of your daydreams a hundred years ago. Are you really this pathetic, Rita?

Yes, I am. I guess I am.

Well, there's a crying shame.

She walks out the door without telling him where she's going. He's glad they understand each other enough for her to forbear insisting that he comfort her for shocking and wounding him. See you later. What shall we have for dinner. How was work. She'll make a sport of her upset, and throw the book in the trash, and go back to the impossible wonderments clogging her head.

He suspects that Rita will report later that she went "out with the girls," her shorthand for falling into one of her drinking binges. Often it's with her co-workers at the Hartlin Foundation, a non-profit company that sends prosthetic limbs to troubled areas. Rita is a shipping coordinator. The Hartlin crews have won worldwide accolades, but on occasion, like everyone else, they have to go out and bitch and moan about what's missing in their lives. She looks the other way when it comes to him, and he does the same, when required, for her.

He met Lillie Roland on such an evening, when his wife had left him alone. He'd gone to an opening night exhibit of Joseph Cornell's shadow boxes at the Museum of Modern Art, where he was arrested by *Untitled (Blue Nude)*. A dream-girl was flying with constellations at her throat, to show that she owned a language of pointed light. He liked the box *Penny Arcade Portrait of Lauren Bacall*. A ball could be set in motion to run over the details of Bacall's life, images from her youth, like a lover coursing over her entirety before returning to the starting place.

Cornell was obsessed with ballerinas, the species that embodies flight, feathers, sex, and travel.

A girl with perfect posture, with honest to God purple eyes and hair the color of a strange dawn, turned to him near the Bacall and said, "Cornell called blue the color of France, and said that women have to be done in blue, because they're like another country."

Maddy has a cold, and Lillie converts the bathroom into a steam palace. She warbles, *If you sing a note high enough, Maddy, you can shatter glass!* Lillie unleashes a note high enough to drill through the ceiling, and Maddy giggles until the steam fills the bottoms of her lungs.

Len bursts in. *Christ! I thought someone was* hurt *in here.*

Lillie's face reddens and her voice shrinks. He's scolding her as if she's a kid he's caught. *No, honey, we're having fun.*

Fun? Then I suppose I'm not wanted.

Lillie goes into the living room to huddle with Len. He's embarrassed. Too bad the landlord won't let them paint the walls cerulean. Lillie draped scarves over the lamps to keep the place from looking bleached. They might be a fire hazard.

She wants to say, Lenny, it's true, you're right, it isn't fair. Maddy should love you better. When I was pregnant, I yelled that I hated her, she was a cancer, a burden. And you never throw that in my face.

And you taught me slowness: Melt into your dance steps, be patient. That alone took me leaps and bounds.

And I've outgrown you, my love.

She can't look at him, she can't talk. But she adjusts the sleeve of his sweater. The salt-scoured air of the Bay moves the dusty blinds.

Sorry, Lil, I must be jumpy.

Don't be sorry, honey. Maddy and I sometimes sail off into space.

Daddy says that everyone used to think that the universe was made of dots. Now people think that the dots are so connected that they're more like strings. Momma's liniment, her shoes, her ribbons—*strings*! Spaghetti—*strings*! Even people are just a lot of strings, except flying really really close together.

Then why does Daddy seem like a dot falling in on itself?

Mark is in Portland to photograph a convention of chefs for *Food & Wine* magazine. From his room at the Sheraton, he phones Lillie. He's never called her at home before. The rain makes silver lines from sky to earth. *Hello?* Her strangely low echoic voice. *Mark?*

How did she guess? Can she read his breathing?

Her name with its three "l"s is like a woman repeatedly en pointe.

He exhales into the phone, unsure of a response. She offers, *I'm touching myself because I can't have you now.*

You can, you can have me, I'm here.

The fright of it, holding hands at the cliff's edge. Shall we jump? How odd longing is—the thing that is only itself by being in excess of itself, the error and the errant building each other higher until you think, *If I knew there would be an end, why did I start?* "Criminal Conversation"—it hits Mark full force. It's not the sex, the lies, or plots that are the crimes so much as daring to insist that speech and desire be in perfect alignment.

She threads a soft cry, a moan into his ear.

I can't bear being this far away, he says.

Motion is marrying what you intend and where you want to be, Mark. That's how to dance. You don't think about going somewhere or hatching some plan, you—lean, I think. You lean to meet yourself where you already are. En pointe, for instance—you pour yourself into the shape of where you belong. Does that make sense?

Yes, everything about her makes perfect sense.

His head rests against the martinized drapes of the Sheraton, with their vague scent of lemon and smoke, though smoking in the room is forbidden, the signs say so.

Len jogs every morning at 5 a.m. on the Marina Green. It is midnight at the wrap party for "The Four Temperaments" by Balanchine, the Sanguinic variations. Tryouts for "Firebird" are next. Lillie is cooing and gossiping after a fourth glass of champagne. A few ballerinas—Bianca and a goose with childish war paint Jesus *they're studiously flamboyant*—are smoking. When he asks them to stop, they stare at him before stubbing out their cigarettes in the plates that held blackberry sorbet and those chocolate tube things with a French name he can never remember, and he wants to shout, *How convenient to have careers that end early!* They are used to him clearing the plates, refilling the glasses, asking interested questions; he's sick of his famous gallantry.

Lillie ignores him. She is speaking French with the husband of the ballerina who owns this house in Cow Hollow. Len recognizes the dissipated smell of Ben-gay and Tiger Balm. A cinnamon-scented candle burns dangerously close to the glass top of the table; is he the only one noticing? A woman with clownish eyeliner says, *Lenny, you've been mute! What's new?*

Lillie and everyone else are suddenly studying him. She's as moony-eyed as when she held up a *Vogue* magazine and said, I covet this dress. *Covet.* As in the ten commandments, which, stop him if he's wrong, has a covet-thing about adultery. Len thought HA, eight thousand dollars for a gown, a fifth of my year's pay, you women are incredible. He's not sure what possesses him, but he launches into the story of his Bavarian Cream Rule.

See, it was my turn to bring the donuts to the teachers' lounge every Monday for a month, and instead of using the lousy ten dollars from the cash fund to buy the plain ones and the dull ones with the sprinkles, I get not one but two boxes of Bavarian Creams and fork out my own money to make up the difference.

Everyone says, "Len, what a treat!" But by the third Monday, I'm not keen on paying over-budget any more, so I come in with the plain ones and the dull sprinkles, and guess what? They're expecting the goddamned Bavarian Creams! You should've seen them, flipping the pink boxes open with one finger and going, "Huh! I can't believe it, Len!"

The ballerinas are getting up and stretching—they do look nice, like elegant hawsers, he admits it—and he's apologizing, and they're saying, No, no, it's late, and goodbye, goodbye, kiss, kiss, and he's in the car with a stony, drunk Lillie.

Lenny? Lenny? Let's say there's a tour bus, and we're going to the cathedral of Chartres—

France again.

Or wherever. Holy shit. We're on a tour bus heading to the ruins of Mazatlan, and the bus breaks down. Do you think, "I'll never get to see Mazatlan, the day is ruined," or do you think, "Now comes an adventure"?

I suppose I'd like the surprise if it turned out to be a good one. How much champagne did you have tonight, Lillie?

Not so much. Let's say there are no promises of that. Let's say the bus is freezing and you're hungry, but you get to huddle or kid around with the couples from Holland and Japan and some sailors on leave from San Diego—and me, maybe I'm there—and Maddy—and the bus driver buys candy from a passing vendor, and that's all? What if that's all? Would you be happy?

We'd get through it. Can you speak plainly? I don't like riddles. (He wants to shout: *If you and Maddy are there, that's the difference.*)

Okay. Remember how we met? In the osteopath's office. I had a bruised kneecap and you had a twisted ankle, but you gave me advice, you came over and found nothing in my cupboard and went to the store and made homemade soup. I'm wondering if we started out with you thinking you had to do every living thing for me, fix everything, and you had to predict absolutely every detail or you'd get mad. Tell me about yourself, Lenny. Why don't you, ever? Is it enough for you, what you do? You're so selfless sometimes that I think you're becoming Self-Less.

Selfless, and Self, Less, that's clever. *Sorry I don't know how to say that in French.*

You bastard. My parents and I spoke French because they're from France. *My father was a baker in Montreal. A* baker. *All right? You sit there sneering at my friends and me. You're the snob.*

218

He knew he'd have to hear again about the humble croissant-baking father. Why can't he censor himself? He's one of the world's spacklers, plastering over gaps and cracks, and if she's the Firebird, she'll sail away on fame, even bite-sized fame, and there'll be nothing to spackle from where he's planted. He wants people to do their work and stop with all the raving yearning. He wants everything to plain *stop*.

But how can he wish Lillie down to earth? That's not why ballerinas are born. *I'm the one who's a success,* he says. *You're the one who hasn't reached where you want to go.*

Maybe you've never heard the expression that there's a higher and higher price to pay for remaining the same.

I don't think you have anything to teach me on that score, Lil, sorry.

He doesn't trust her to have the courage to see his courage as she leaves him. He's a good teacher because he senses when it's time for children to rise onward. He still loves her. She's weeping and he puts an arm around her. *Stop crying, Lillie. Dear. We're two nice people. That's not a crime. Is there something you want to tell me? No? Not yet? Don't feel terrible. It happens all the time, marrying the wrong man. But I don't know how much more I can take. You turned a corner, and you liked it so much you turned again, then again, until now you're going in a circle, and you've left it to me to say, Go in a straight line. I'll watch until you're a vanishing point, because I can't not watch you.*

Maddy draws people as insects. Teddy MacPherson is a pill bug, Mrs. Arneson is a bee, Maddy is a praying mantis with ruby eyes and green limbs. A string goes from

Momma to somewhere outside. Maddy wants to find the end of the string to hold onto Momma.

Your spine is a pole connected to the sky, Maddy.

Momma curls up on Maddy's bed with her and copies a line from Shakespeare and pins it to the wall alongside Maddy's school papers with their gold stars: *Light seeking light doth light of light beguile.* She says, Repeat that until it's inside you, Maddy, and never mind that you don't know what it means yet; some day you will. But be very sad if there comes a day when you imagine that you understand it all.

Len senses a breakthrough with Martin. The boy tries to speak. Len has asked the class: *Where does the moon go during daylight?* The blank stares, the lips being chewed, the waiting-for-the-teacher-to-give-the-answer.

Martin points upward. He jabs a finger toward the windows.

Yes! Martin! Good! It stays right there in the sky! We just can't see it when there's light! The moon never leaves!

Len's pulse quickens; soon Martin will form a sentence. He waits. Not yet. But soon.

Is it only ten minutes later that the world changes so horribly? That fast? Connie D'Allessandro wets her pants during naptime. The children erupt. They blow sky-high. *Connie is a baby, it's a flood and I'm drowning, baby, BABY!*

Martin screams, *C-C-C-Connie w-w-wet her P-P-PANTS! C-C-Connie wet her p-p-p-PANTS!* He is beside himself. The kids are making fun of someone else! He begins to dance, to writhe; Len wonders if he's having a seizure and runs to contain him, but he won't quit that infernal *C-C-Connie.* He bites Len's hand covering his

вий, в ко... по... ...ист... ...и дея-
...р...я», [1] —
...ав... ...ри... ...тезис
...ость» ...то... ......тезис,
сделав ег... ...тиво-
речия во ... ...п... ...я его
только ли... ...ысшей
степени с... ...иаль-
ных влия... ...опре-
деляли ... ...ичных
слоев р... ...ф... ...о доре-
волюци...

Ита... ...о...
постоя... ...к
попыти... ...к...
«узел ... ...о...
и изу... н... ...ге...
точки... ...
когда... ...о... ...: «Чело-
век, ...пр... ...жен для
на... ...ет... ...до...я, на-
ни... со стр... силой, — все
...от его рели-
...про-
...оцесс
...ений.
...х по-
...венно
...даже
...все-
...ойное
...вме-
...а.
...ытки,
...желал
...й тен-

...альней-
...м тома

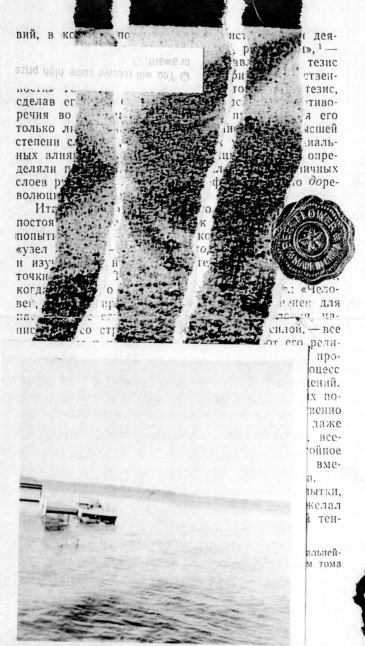

FIG. 8. *Make my coffin white after the dance; adorn it with garlands; remember me; flying now, I shall never forget you.*

mouth—nothing must stifle his delight in someone else's agony.

Washing off the blood from Martin's bite, with Connie remanded to the principal so she can go home for dry clothing, away from the howls, Len decides he is done with the arrogance of picturing himself as more above-it-all than the other teachers. He cannot shake a clear, horrific vision of Lillie bouncing up and down on some guy's enormous hard-on. She's staring into his eyes, out of her hide on fire. The guy is all over her bare ass from behind, hissing, *I'm glad you love it this way.* Len puts his head under the running faucet. He must tell Maddy that her drawings of people as insects have a serious flaw; they have insects' faces instead of human ones.

Lillie has auditioned for the Firebird and bought champagne. That's how well she thinks it went, though she won't know for a few days, and she wants to spend time, as much time as time allows, with Mark, until the winner is announced. *Suzanne Farrell used to remark that when she danced it was like watching Balanchine in her limbs. Patricia MacBride said that when Balanchine designed a dance for you, you fell in love with him all over again.* Has Mark really done this for her, with the strength of his love? Like a partner lifting her on stage.

She has a way of sitting with her knees together and slanted to the side, like a girl at a school dance. Look at her eyes, look at her containing the future she wants to keep slightly longer at bay, to keep enjoying its approach: Firebird. A wet star is on her silk shift from her setting the champagne bottle between her knees to pull out the cork.

Mark is startled at how one-way his vision has been; he's the one lifted, she's the one in his limbs, so he begins slowly at first and builds with a *What if . . . ?* speech, unrehearsed: He'll take care of her and Maddy, he'll give them a home, she's said herself that she's afraid of what's to come, and it's time to—

But she's staring at him. He feels like the-much-older-man-with-no-more-years-to-waste.

You sound just like Len! *I'm awful to him! Ungrateful! Here I am with you*—

Mark is ready to say, *That's right, you're with me, so why not keep that,* but Lillie is on her feet with her champagne glass and is screaming, and the glass hits the headboard of the bed and shatters and a piece like a sharp eggshell cuts her hand, which he grabs, shouting, *What is this for? What are you doing?*

He carries her across the room to the sink, her feet off the floor and kicking, and the water goes pink with her blood. Mark's saying, *Lillie, Lillie, I only want us to be happy,* but she combusts, she shrieks, he can barely contain her and keep her hand under the stream, *Happiness? Was he like everyone else, thinking that love was the same as happiness? Happiness is* marriage *and that's why both of them were happy where they were, happy marriages were a dime a dozen, and that's why he had one and so did she, marriage meant scraping up only enough sex, and that's if you were lucky, to be medicinal and alleviate the wildest need for it, and what Mark was suggesting was that he and she now had the strength for jealousy and inflicting the type of anguish that made you stop and ask yourself what the hell you were doing, and then would come the fright of not knowing anything except that you couldn't stop, and if he wanted happiness then he might think about leaving her alone because what they had was—*

Shh. Lillie. Let me take you to the emergency.

The cut was deep enough to require three stitches. Her hand bandaged, she leaned against him and made a joke about not thinking she could look any paler than usual. It was late; she was overdue at home. She took loss and marked herself with it, drew blood, registered injury—something exacted from the flesh. Lillie was a physical animal, wearing factually what they had between them. He didn't know what showed on him.

She's kissing him, saying she's torn to pieces.

Sorry, sorry. My love! Your poor hand. Never mind. There's only you and me, I mean right now in the car, it's all all right. Isn't it. We have time, we have every inch of the time we want.

He lets her out to catch her streetcar. *Lillie? Congratulations on your audition. I'm sure you'll be the Firebird.*

He watches as she looks back to wave from the street. He'd spoken too soon. It wasn't easy to leave a husband who cheered her on so graciously, with her too young still to know that generosity can signal a lack in the person offering it. Mark was part of her general disengagement; soon she would be aware that she was beginning the work of dislodging from her mistake in marrying Len—or rather, she had yet to learn how to forgive herself for inflicting overt pain. Mark might be the first phase of her lesson, not necessarily its outcome. When he had been younger, he had not known how to listen to anyone warning him that by settling for the male ideal of the best of both worlds—Rita's offer of marriage and freedom—he would not have either of them entire and complete.

Mrs. Arneson often assigns Maddy Chase to help other children with their reading, writing, and math. Daddy says that when he was a schoolboy, children like Maddy got called "the Steamships," and ones like Teddy MacPherson were "the Tugboats." Your name got put on a cutout picture of the kind of boat you were, and it was pinned to a bulletin board. Steamships were supposed to guide Tugboats.

She grins at Teddy MacPherson's homework.

Oh, Teddy! You've written S-U-R-L-Y instead of S-U-R-E-L-Y! Maybe because you're surely surly?

Maddy sees Crystal Roma in a neon green sweater across the playground of Galileo Elementary. She's eager to tell her friend some exciting news. Last night, her mother explained that a ballerina could know the dance steps precisely and still lose an audition. The difference will be in the *feeling*—Maddy had no idea that such a thing could show! Momma was joyful but tired from an audition; she must have given it "her all" because her hand was hurt, and Daddy made French onion soup because Momma adores it, and he taught Maddy how to build a real fire in the fireplace . . . Momma showing her those dance steps *with feeling*, Maddy leaping, Daddy applauding them both, the fire yellow and blue and red going up and up in big tattered tongues—

What just happened?

Maddy staggers and sees Teddy MacPherson being thrown to the ground and Mrs. Arneson screeching.

Stars, blurred ones, drop down to the stage. Crystal Roma races toward her; Maddy blooms with a love of love,

225

a burst of feeling but not the way it usually hits; it comes the way it did last night, when you begin to see you can wear it on your flesh, that it isn't always a dream.

révérence

Lillie isn't sure whether to be amused or worried as she reads the note that Len has scrawled on a torn section of a brown shopping bag: *Gone to Tommy's Joynt.* It's unlike him not to be home right now, after school. Last night's family amusements were of course a sweet farce. Lillie's bandaged hand throbs. She sits, pretending that she isn't waiting for the telephone to ring, with Andre Phillips, the company's creative director, on the other end, telling her that she's the Firebird. She's been hazy on the subject of what exactly she expects of Mark, and vagueness is not in a ballerina's training. Imprecision is as bad as a broken leg. She's been floating along, insisting that events present themselves in such a manner that a decision decides itself, but maybe it's time to put events in motion by her own decisions. But she does love Lenny. He's not a drinker, and she grieves to think of him swilling the beers-from-around-the-world at Tommy's, joining the line for the buffalo stew, staring at the ceiling with its bicycles, puppets, and banners, like a child's mad playhouse.

Compassion is hardly love.

The phone trills. She allows it two rings, like a teenage girl trying not to appear anxious.

She won't recollect driving to Saint Francis Memorial; she wishes herself there, and it is there she appears, flying down the white corridors, hollering, *Maddy! Maddy! I'm here! I won't ever leave you!*

She hears (or isn't it Lillie's mind issuing the cry, since Maddy is in surgery?), *Momma! Where are you?*

The press is pouring in; the TV cameras want their indecent shots; the police are circling. Maddy will need her knee replaced, a Teflon joint. Months of therapy might have her walking at half-speed, and thereafter her spirit may determine how fully she recovers.

Len is soused when he arrives at the hospital. Lillie puts her arm around him and marches him into the men's room. She will stay glued to his side. For once in his life, he's drunk, he's picked the worst possible day for it, but she won't let the reporters sniff the beer on him. *I'll take care of you, Lenny, nothing is fair, it's usually you that's home, you would have gotten the call and been the hero first at her side, it isn't fair.*

Lemon verbena is a fine tea for the nerves. Infusions from the sharp, thin leaves yield an acidic bite but also a gentleness that carries you off to sleep. A policeman will escort them through the cordons of the press when they arrive at Saint Francis Memorial. The story is spreading like wildfire. Len braids Lillie's hair and changes the bandage on her hand and abandons his plan to ask how her injury occurred. Her good hand shakes and she sobs that it's vain to be putting on eyeliner, she throws the black pencil in the sink, but Len says, Lillie, go ahead and look put-together. Maddy adores you that way. So do I.

Len keeps along in this fashion, slow and steady, until his skin is crawling: He is monstrous with his sense of purpose—it's wrong, it's too much like peace. He wraps himself in tasks, they make a fat rubber suit he can vanish inside, and there'll be Taskmaster Heaven for years now, what with Maddy's knee.

He does not admit to Lillie that this morning he drove to the office of the City Ballet to meet with Andre Phillips. *You're about to decide the principal dancer for Firebird, and forgive my imposition and don't tell Lillie I'm here, but I'm sure you've heard what's happened to my wife and me, about our girl. I want to assure you, Sir, that she'll be able to dance. It will give Lillie a reason to live, and it will give our baby one, too, if her mother is the Firebird, this nightmare won't affect her ability to—*

Take it easy, Len. We've already decided. Lillie's got it. It's hers, if she wants it.

She does. She does. It would mean the world to me. Thank you.

Lillie picks up a bouquet of asters that she'll set on Maddy's bedside table. As Len escorts her to the car, he wants to tell her of the decision but his own folly keeps him mute. *I'll take care of everything, Lillie, don't worry, I'll make you happy.* No wonder Andre sneered at him. What possessed him to beg like that, as if Lillie didn't deserve the role but needed some charity to cheer herself up.

Len adjusts the rear view mirror. He says, *Go talk to him, Lil.*

What?

Go talk to him, Lillie. I'd hate the thought of losing you, too. Go on, so I don't have to punch him out.

Lenny?

I teach five year olds, but that doesn't mean I am one. If you want to get into the car with him—

I'll be right back, Len. We're due at the hospital.

One Must Speak of Sex in French

Lillie leans through Mark's open window. This late, this late, a first: He has never come to her home. There's so much she wants to tell him. *My love,* she says. And then speech leaves her. It has deserted him. His eyes are sapphires. It is pointless to add: You and me, we are so far past happiness.

relevés devant

Not true, the gossip going on, says Bianca.

What are people saying?

Nothing, says Bianca. *Congratulations.*

Lillie knows the rumor. She hears the whispers. She didn't get the Firebird because she was better than Bianca; Maddy got it for her. Maddy's accident put Lillie in the national (and overseas) news—and what a draw, what (unfortunate though it is, a real tragedy) great advance publicity. Plus now she has the fierceness, the shock, the vehemence to be the Firebird. That part of it may be true. Or perhaps none of it is.

Maddy will be home soon. *Momma, won't you and Daddy take care of me?*

Yes, darling. Whyever did you think we wouldn't?

The reviews of Lillie Roland as the Firebird with the San Francisco City Ballet are excellent; ecstatic, in places. Mark is forced to notice flyers in the mail with her face and name. He sees an advertisement nailed to a phone pole. *Lillie Roland takes her former shy grace and unlocks hidden reserves. She did of course recently suffer a horrid misfortune . . .*

Mark buys a solo ticket to see the performance but is too distracted to follow the story. Lillie wears a strange topknot, like a feathered lightning rod, and her arms go rigid when fighting death, but in her partner's arms, her fury spent, she collapses: She cannot win! She cannot win!

Where did he go with her, where did he take her inside the little room with its posters of Paris? The artist Joseph Cornell did not know physical love until he was old, and though he was too far gone with unmet desire to penetrate a woman, he wrote in his diary about *soixante-neuf* and *Je voudrais . . .* He had awaited actual love for so long that when it finally arrived, he declared that he could only write about it in the language of the country of love.

Mark Galway stares through the darkness. Soon his ache will transfigure into an understanding that this is how events were fated to play out: Lillie there, in agony, wearing his desperate want of her—wearing the final gift he has unwittingly given her, as she plays the tormented, imperiled bird—the gift of usable grief.

He leaves before the encore. In the cold on Grove Street, before the crowds pour out, he hails a cab to go home. A great new photograph no doubt awaits him, now that he is back to being pierced alive, back to being among the walking wounded, back with the human race, but the difference between now and when he was a young hotshot is that he would trade this future acclaimed photograph in a heartbeat for her.

Rita Galway resolves again to give up drinking. After a three-wine lunch, she filled out an order form incorrectly, and the prosthetic body parts got shipped to her office rather than overseas. She deals in glass eyes, arms and legs, curved steel for feet, hooks for hands, jellied sacs for gouged-out torsos. Her job is to help make flesh whole in teeming, forgotten places, Cambodia, Sierra Leone, Angola. Mark's Belfast.

Where is he? It's eleven o'clock at night. She sits in their living room awaiting his key in the lock.

He enters and sinks into a chair next to her on the sofa and puts his elbows on the armrests and folds his hands in front of himself.

Rita is tempted to say, You've been out making a fool of yourself.

But she doesn't. He has finally arrived at the place where she's always been. She reaches over and rests her palm on his clenched hands. They'll get along, argue, go places, run errands, chat about work, now that he's as ridiculous as she is over something impossible. It's not nothing that they have, this bond based upon accretion. Now he will move at the same speed that gets her through her own days, as if through water. In water you can have a screaming fight and not hear a word. You can try striking a blow, but the punches are cushioned; there's not much that can hurt you anymore.

To her surprise, he opens his fist to grasp the hand she's offering.

So she says, Today at work I got another of those calls, Mark. You know, from some dismembered ghost, some damaged soul overseas, and this one said in his broken English, *I owe you my life for my arm; now I have a hand that must if you please clasp yours.* It hit me that in every foreign language, the thank-you sounds *obliged*, not merely grateful. Not our American way of checking an acknowledgment off a list to be done with it. They've got something missing forever, but they're dying to say, If you ever come to the land where I am, I'll do everything I can think of for you, and it won't ever be enough.

It's good that you make a difference, he says.

Marriage causes the ultimate creolized language.

Madeleine Chase (she prefers her grown-up name now) decides that both pain and pleasure are a throb. At first, she dislikes the drugs she must take because they blur all lines, everywhere. But while walking in the Sunset District, often stopping on her crutches, she enjoys seeing the pain melt into a vision of colors radiating from the homes, the buildings. Yellows, greens, pinks; the roofs turn into the prettiest barbed wire.

At home, dizzy, Madeleine draws the homes from memory, in pictures like jagged gardens. Because she is famous—she's been on television and in the newspapers, internationally—because of her permanent injury, her artwork is in museums and finds its way to the covers of magazines.

Fame! What a joke!

That's nothing! Nothing! She has everyone bamboozled!

It will be a true artwork when she can bring herself to draw her quiet father—solid bands of primary colors, but with the edges torn.

It will be a masterpiece when she can draw her beguiling mother. *Momma, Momma, where is it that you go when you close your eyes?*

Madeleine will paint her as light seeking light.

But what does that look like?

Does it vanish when you try to capture it?

Are you burned alive if you find it?

Final Notes

We stop abruptly at one point and stare over our shoulders at a gap where we seemed to have lost years, a Rip Van Winkle spate—or is it living in the tale of Sleeping Beauty? I thought I was living and working as usual, but my book preceding this one was a decade ago. In that time, I turned sixty. My beloved father died; I got married. I settled farther into my life in New York City, though almost everything I write centers upon my native California.

Reading over these stories, all published a while back, I wondered if I should update them. In the title story, Nathan, who endured the war in Vietnam, consults a phonebook, not Facebook, to locate Mrs. Violet Delmar, and even in his own era, his calibrating of light-board images to effect animation becomes, to his riveted dismay, archaic.

In "A Simple Affair," a couple with modest salaries contemplates buying a house in the Mission District of San Francisco! My characters read print media. There are no cellphones, much less smart-phones; people get lost and have no GPS. They watch *60 Minutes* and talk about Braille and recall the tanks rolling into Prague. They search for voices via the blinking red light of answering machines.

Finally, though, the stories we invent are records of our time, and so I leave them standing as they were and are. My publishers simply read and loved them without qualification, and they have given me a fresh boost, air and lift to the rescue. I'm a writer revived. I thank them deeply.

Much as I'm tempted to call my husband, Christopher Cerf, a dream, he has been my loving and supportive reality to an enormous degree, compounding my publishers' faith. My parents raised me, and my five siblings, to follow our hearts, and I remain grateful to my widowed mother, Elizabeth Vaz, and to the memory of my father, August Mark Vaz.

Thanks to my agent, Eleanor Jackson of Dunow, Carlson & Lerner, and thanks also to Elizabeth Strout, Varley O'Connor, Patricia Duffy, Maria Konnikova Hamilton, Rebecca Goldstein, Miguel Vaz, Tayari Jones, Major Jackson, Alexander Chee & Dustin Schell, Julia Glass & Dennis Cowley, and Cindy & Denis Johnson for their sustaining friendships.

Acknowledgments

These stories, some in slightly different forms, first appeared in the following publications:

"Bébé Marie Springs from the Box," *ACM (Another Chicago Magazine)*; "Blue Flamingo Looks at Red Water" *(The Sun)*; "East Bay Grease" *(The Antioch Review)*; "the rice artist" *(The Iowa Review)*; "The Glass Eaters" *(Glimmer Train)*; "Scalings" *(The Gettysburg Review)*; "My Family, Posing for Rodin" *(The Antioch Review)*; "A Simple Affair" *(Gargoyle)*; "Utter" *(The Malahat Review)*; "The Love Life of an Assistant Animator" *(Glimmer Train)*; "One Must Speak of Sex in French" *(Confrontation)*.

"Blue Flamingo Looks at Red Water," "East Bay Grease," "The Glass Eaters," and "The Love Life of an Assistant Animator" are Audible Books, available through Audible.com.

About the Author

KATHERINE VAZ is the author of two novels, *Saudade,* a Barnes & Noble Discover Great New Writers selection, and *Mariana,* translated into six languages and picked by the Library of Congress as one of the Top Thirty International Books of 1998. *Fado & Other Stories* received a Drue Heinz Literature Prize, and *Our Lady of the Artichokes & Other Portuguese-American Stories* won a Prairie Schooner Book Award. Her short fiction has appeared in many magazines, and her children's stories have been included in anthologies by Viking, Penguin, and Simon & Schuster.

Vaz was a Briggs-Copeland Fellow in Fiction at Harvard University (2003-9) and a Fellow of the Radcliffe Institute for Advanced Study (2006-7). She has been awarded a National Endowment for the Arts Fellowship and a Harman Fellowship and has lectured internationally about Portuguese and Luso-American literature as well as magical realism.

A native Californian, she lives in New York City and East Hampton with her husband, Christopher Cerf, an editor, composer, television producer, and author.

CPSIA information can be obtained
at www.ICGtesting.com
Printed in the USA
LVOW08s1813150617
538254LV00003B/539/P